About the Author

Bill Hatfield has been a practicing certified public accountant since 1975. He has his own CPA practice. He has been a certified financial planner, held multiple securities licenses and was a branch manager for Raymond James. He served on the board of directors of the New York State Society and on multiple committees of the society.

United States vs David Mattson

Bill Hatfield

United States vs David Mattson

Olympia Publishers
London

www.olympiapublishers.com
OLYMPIA PAPERBACK EDITION

Copyright © Bill Hatfield 2024

The right of Bill Hatfield to be identified as author of
this work has been asserted in accordance with sections 77 and 78 of
the Copyright, Designs and Patents Act 1988.

All Rights Reserved

No reproduction, copy or transmission of this publication
may be made without written permission.
No paragraph of this publication may be reproduced,
copied or transmitted save with the written permission of the publisher,
or in accordance with the provisions
of the Copyright Act 1956 (as amended).

Any person who commits any unauthorised act in relation to
this publication may be liable to criminal
prosecution and civil claims for damage.

A CIP catalogue record for this title is
available from the British Library.

ISBN: 978-1-83543-086-6

This is a work of fiction. Any resemblance to actual persons, living or
dead, is purely coincidental.

First Published in 2024

Olympia Publishers
Tallis House
2 Tallis Street
London
EC4Y 0AB

Printed in Great Britain

Dedication

I would like to dedicate this book to my family, Ellie, my wife, and my four children, Marcus, Heather, Joseph and Elizabeth. Without their support and help, I would have imploded.

Acknowledgments

I want to thank David Hazard, my friend and writing coach; without his help, this book would never have been born.

The Order

The event came out of nowhere—literally, out of a clear blue sky—and altered everything. Americans had no idea whatsoever all that would change for them. After the foreign terrorist forces tried to penetrate their lives came other forces, closer to home. Much closer.

George W. Bush was inaugurated as President on January 20, 2001; less than nine months later, he became a wartime Commander-in-Chief when four commercial aircraft were hijacked by Al-Qaeda terrorists and flown into the World Trade Center, the Pentagon, and a field in the township of Stoney Creek, Pennsylvania. That day, 2,996 people died in the attack and over 6,000 more were injured. Many more would suffer the effects for years, including long-term illness, disability, and even eventual death.

During President Bush's address to the nation on the evening of the attack, he said, "We will make no distinction between the terrorists who committed these acts and those who harbor them."

The message was clear. All supporters of terrorism would be rooted out and punished.

John Ashcroft had also been in office for only months when the September 11, 2001 terrorist attack occurred. In its aftermath, the Department of Homeland Security was founded. The Patriot Act was passed less than a month after the attack, which gave the FBI and the justice department broad powers to detain and interrogate citizens who could be a possible source of potential terrorist threats. United States citizens could now be surveilled in order to detect terrorism.

Not long after the head of the FBI, Robert Mueller, John Ashcroft, President Bush, and Vice President Dick Cheney met in the Oval Office to discuss the tragedy and what was to be done in response to the event. Neither Mueller nor Ashcroft were looking forward to the meeting. FBI Director Mueller knew the Bureau had not done an adequate job of defending the United States, resulting in the 9/11 attacks.

As the president entered the Oval Office, all three in attendance stood as per protocol. President Bush was clearly not a happy man. His face was distorted with anger and the people in the oval office were about to feel his wrath.

President Bush took his place at the head of the two couches in the back of the office. He gave a short presentation to the attendees, making his position clear. At the end, he turned to Mueller and placed much of the responsibility on the FBI. The FBI's primary mission is to protect the United States against terrorist and foreign intelligence threats. The president made it clear the FBI had failed miserably in its assigned task. The comments were not unexpected. The president then said, "I want any and all possible or potential terrorists detained and interrogated to clean up any future threats of attack."

Turning to Ashcroft, he clearly laid out what he expected going forward regarding the position of the justice department. The president said, "John, any and all leads given to the justice department are to be prosecuted and punished. There should be no negotiated plea bargains. Further, he would look to the judicial system of the U.S. to abide by the sentencing guidelines and show no departures from them."

Ashcroft nodded, forcing from his mind the fact that this

mandate was not legal. Sentencing guidelines were not mandatory. Now, however, sitting judges and possible candidates would be informed that they were going to be monitored for compliance.

The stage was now set for a large dragnet to be thrown out over the U.S. and all its citizens.

*

Sarah, the young teller, was at her assigned position at the front counter in the Saratoga, New York, branch of the Bank of America. All newbies had to do a month on the teller line, and she expected another long day of boredom. The customer traffic was not intense, especially in the first hour after opening, and she yawned as she performed the mundane duties on her list.

Her second customer of the day was Yusuf Abdulla, a man with a broad smile, a full black beard, and very dark eyes.

"I need a check in the amount of nine-thousand and five-hundred dollars. Please make it payable to Assad Trading Company from my Bread for Children account at the bank." He slid a piece of paper across the counter to her, with the number of the account on it.

Accessing the account on her computer, she saw the account had over $400,000 in it. She prepared the check and had him wait while she got it authorized by an officer. When she gave the check to Yusuf, she watched until he was out the door.

The transfer of large amounts was a trigger, and looking at Abdulla's account history, she had seen there were thirteen withdrawals, each for just under $10,000.

Placing the closed sign at her window, she walked across the lobby and knocked at the branch manager's office door. When he looked up, she said, "I need to show you something. Take a look at this account," and she told him the number.

When he pushed back from his computer, he nodded. "You were right to flag this. Fill this out." He handed her a blank *Suspicious Activity Report* form. "Give it to the compliance officer when he comes in."

With a few strokes of the pen, the young teller set in motion events with far-reaching consequences.

Chapter 1

Dave Mattson finished his half-hour run on the treadmill at home when a text came in from his assistant.

"He's phoned twice. Very agitated when I said you're not in yet."

He texted back.

"Thanks for the heads-up."

Dave knew who *he* was. A good client, but sometimes high-pressured. Of course, his questions and needs were important, but no one was bleeding out here. He could wait. Showering and dressing, he reminded himself that 99.9 percent of his clients were respectful and patient. This guy, a highly respected heart surgeon, was in the point-one percent who thought his needs were more important than everyone else's. Dave could imagine him imperiously bossing around nurses and interns.

So, yeah, he could wait, even if he believed his needs were of far-reaching, international importance.

*

Walking up the sidewalk to his office in a large Victorian home a block off the city's main street, he felt pride at what he'd accomplished in just three years. Dave had bought the old house reasonably and had sunk a lot of money into improvements. As a result, the property value went way up. Now, in addition to his certified public accounting business, he also had a booming financial planning and investment venture, as well. It wasn't just the renovation that gave him pride, but also the fact that with careful, conservative planning, he'd maneuvered through some recent downs in the economy and still come out way ahead. His ability to produce results like this, taking a conservative but canny approach to investing, was the reason his clients trusted him and he wanted to keep it that way. All you had in this business was your reputation. That was his most prized possession.

Inside, his assistant, Jen, handed him a small sheaf of messages.

"One from your wife."

"Already? Hannah's hardly had time to get to her office."

The message wasn't urgent; just a reminder.

"One from your daughter."

"It's about final wedding plans, am I right?"

Jen smiled. "You guessed it."

The third message was from his largest client, who was in the middle of a difficult, complex federal income tax audit. "I'd better get to him right away."

"As soon as you deal with Mr. Impatient in there."

Dave looked at her questioningly.

"You know who I mean."

"He's in my office? Did you tell him I am busy and my schedule is packed?"

"He charged in right after I texted you and insisted on seeing you right away. Even more rude than usual. I think he's wearing a hole in the carpet with his pacing."

"My good friend!" Dr. Yusuf Abdullah greeted him.

"Friend" was a stretch. They had a business relationship going back over twenty years, and Abdullah had a suite of medical offices here in Saratoga Springs, not far from Dave and Hannah's home. To say he had a strong personality, the kind that pushes people away, was an understatement. He was so intense that Dave wondered if he was that way on purpose, so people would keep their distance. Nonetheless, over the years they had developed a good working relationship, made stronger when Yusuf had a potentially difficult IRS audit one year in which Dave cleared him of any wrongdoing. After that, Yusuf relied on him more and more. Having a deep look into Yusuf's finances had convinced Dave he was a man of honor—even if he could be a pain in the ass sometimes. Like right now.

Dave dropped his briefcase on the desk. "What's up?"

"I need you to file a not-for-profit application with the IRS for a new entity— Bread for Children Foundation. Some friends are trying to establish it for the people of Kuwait, who were seriously affected by the Iraqi incursions. So many are economically and medically deprived, and people are starving, as well. Help is urgently needed. Can you do this right away?"

"Other people can help you with this," Dave responded. "I am swamped now, and I'm over my head."

"I tried to work with a woman in Albany. She was supposed to be a specialist in this area, but she was difficult."

Dave tried not to smile at that.

"I need *you* to help me. You're a good man, and I trust you completely."

He wished Yusuf had not pressed that button. The trust of his clients was something he highly prized. Still, he didn't want to give the impression that Yusuf could pressure him into doing his bidding.

"I can recommend someone else, who's excellent."

Yusuf pulled a picture from his suitcoat pocket of Kuwaiti

and Kurdish refugees, showing them hunkered down in makeshift tents. "You see, over here in America, you and I will go home to warm houses tonight and enjoy full bellies. These people are sleeping in the cold, and parents are giving up what little food they have—just scraps, really—to feed their starving children. Look at this father holding his little girl." He tapped the photo.

Dave hated this. He was a sucker for helping people, and the image of a father, face drawn in grief, holding his listless little daughter, punched him in the heart. He suspected Yusuf had known it would.

"Imagine if this were your beautiful daughter, may she be blessed."

"Look, okay. I'll work it in. But you and your friends have to give me exactly the information I need. I'll give you a list. It's long."

"Whatever you need, my friend. We'll give it."

"Did he even say thank you?" Jen asked, after Dave saw Yusuf out the door.

"What do you think?"

"Did you hold off whatever he was demanding?"

Dave grinned.

"How on earth are you going to take on one more thing? You've got a stack of tax season work already *and* a wedding coming up fast."

"I'll give it to Mary."

"Is it something she can handle? She's new. Eager to learn, but new."

"It's a bit beyond her, but I'll work with her on it."

Jen shook her head. "When in your sleep?"

*

Just before noon, Richard Andrews tapped on the office door.

Dave barely looked up from a stack of files. "How are things in tax attorney land?"

"Busy, as I'm sure you are. Let's go to lunch. I need a martini."

"I need to have lunch brought in. I can hardly shovel my way through this pile."

"You look half-whipped and it's only lunchtime. Let's get out of here. I'm buying."

"Well, that's a first." Dave dropped his pen. "Okay, I'm getting a headache anyway. I'm in." He was only too happy to be relieved of the overwhelming pressures of the office this time of year. A short break with a buddy would be great.

The Saratoga Race Track's Turf Restaurant was packed, but playing their friendship and client cards with the *maître d'* got them a seat overlooking the flat track just outside a sunny window. The track had just opened for the season, and two jockeys were working out horses, one chestnut and one coal black.

"I hope you didn't want privacy." Richard laughed, surveying the other tables. "Between the two of us, we probably know most of the people in here."

It was true. Dave recognized maybe a third of the lunch crowd. "As long as I don't run into one client in particular."

"Let me guess. Yusuf Abdullah."

Dave shook his head. "That guy. Damn."

"He can be unbearably rude when he wants something done. I don't get it, though. At other times, he can be compassionate and so kind. Anyone I've ever known who was a patient of his

19

thinks he hangs the sun, moon and stars," said Richard.

The waiter came for their drink orders.

Dave put down the menu. "I gotta tell you. He barged into my office this morning, crushed my schedule, and got me off to a rough start."

"What was the dire emergency?"

"Some non-profit humanitarian organization that friends of his want him to start."

"You, see? That's the thing about that guy. He's got a heart of gold. He just goes about getting what he wants all wrong. Good motive. Lousy presentation."

"You're right. He's a good man. I need to let it go. Anyway, I'll help him out."

"That's because you're a good man, too. A lot of guys don't like him and would have punted him out of their office."

Richard's Martini had disappeared quickly and he started a political rant. Dave had no interest in entertaining. But there he was, stuck and nodding. After Richard drained the first round, he ventured into territory that made Dave even more uncomfortable.

"Ya know that guy, Yusuf, is just like all of the rest of them."

"Easy," Dave replied, sipping his iced tea. "The gin and vermouth are kicking in."

"It's true. All Middle Easterners are pushy."

"C'mon, Richard, stop. Have you tried out the new golf clubs you got for Christmas?"

That helped.

"You're worried I'm gonna bury you on the course this year, aren't you?"

Ironic, Dave thought, *how obnoxious Richard could be while criticizing someone—in fact, a whole ethnic group.*

While Richard ordered another martini and talked about golf

handicaps and how often he'd beat everyone on the course with him, Dave's mind went elsewhere. He wondered how much prejudice Yusuf and his wife encountered here in well-to-do, white-bread Saratoga Springs.

Yusuf and Salma, his wife, had moved to the Springs in early 1981, and Yusuf established his surgical practice. Word spread around the social circles that he was born in Iraq, raised and educated in Bagdad. He and Salma both became U.S. citizens, and proudly displayed the American flag outside their posh home and his office. There was a wrinkle.

Yusuf became very active in the Muslim community, and eyebrows went up. Some of the women welcomed Salma into their homes and clubs; others made an obviously shallow pretense of it.

"I can't for the life of me figure out why we allow anyone into this country who's from a terrorist nation," Richard said, getting loud. "As far as I'm concerned, they're all terrorists at heart."

A number of heads turned, a few nodded. Others turned away in disgust.

"You know all the nine-eleven attackers were from Saudi Arabia—our good, oil-supplying buddies—right? And you know there are good, hardworking, law-abiding Muslims, right?"

The waiter arrived with their lunch orders.

"Aren't they all just the same, though? They all hate us."

Dave knew a rant about Sharia law was probably coming next, and he needed a diversion.

"Hey, I need to eat fast and get back to work. Your grilled steak salad looks great. Why don't you tuck into it before it gets cold?"

The damage had been done to Dave's break from work,

though, and his mind was stuck on post 9/11 realities and Yusuf Abdullah.

After the horrors of September 2001, the U.S. Government forbade trade and any financial transactions with Iraq. The restrictions became known as Iraqi Sanctions Regulations. There was to be no trade with Iraq or direct or indirect transfer of funds to Iraq. As a result of these sanctions and others imposed by the United Nations, the people of Iraq experienced food shortages and severe malnutrition. The pictures of listless children lying in the arms of weeping parents were heart-wrenching.

Dave wondered, *Did loud mouths like Richard ever consider how much help the Iraqi people gave the U.S. in toppling Saddam Hussein's despotic, murderous regime? How did that make them "all alike" haters of America?*

*

At the end of the afternoon, Dave had a headache. Even so, he stopped by a nursing facility on his way home to visit his oldest client and longtime friend of the family, Evelyn Martin, ninety-six and still spry, but with no family nearby.

"What are you doing here?" Evelyn chided him. "You look like you need to go home and have a Manhattan."

"I'm a lightweight. A cocktail would knock me on my rear end right now."

"Next time you come by, bring me some scotch in a flask." She nodded toward the orderlies on duty. "They won't suspect a thing, and I'll sleep better. I'm waking up at midnight and lying there awake all night."

"Hey, I'm there too."

"What's keeping you up at night?"

He didn't want to burden her with the list. The business, family demands, home and office expenses. "Who knows, Evelyn? Tell me how you're doing?"

An hour later, when he walked in the door at home, Hannah was in the living room, holding their Shih-Tzu. Frankie jumped down and came over to jump at him, begging for a walk.

"You look beat. Frankie, get down. Stop. Did you stop to see Evelyn again?"

He undid his tie, thinking about having a shot of scotch after all, but it really would put him out and he knew Hannah needed to talk. "She's ninety-six and going strong. She'll outlive me."

"She will if you don't slow down. You're spread way too thin."

During dinner, Hannah set her fork down. "I feel bad bringing this up, but..."

He smiled at her. "I know. Daisy's wedding. Tell me what's on your mind. Do you need more cash?"

"No David."

David, not Dave. This was serious.

"I need more of *you*. So does Daisy."

He put down his fork. "Hey, I'm sorry. I know I've been distracted."

She reached over and squeezed his hand.

"I know you're very busy now and that Dr. Abdullah has a good cause, but he keeps putting more and more pressure on you."

"He's the last thing I need right now, and I need to do something to get him off my back."

"I'm doing my best to protect you from more demands. I can see how distracted you are. But we need to discuss how you're going to fit yourself into Daisy's wedding. I mean the day before and the day after. I've made all the plans and arrangements. But it's time for you to step up and involve yourself."

He was surprised at his own response, which he fought to contain. He had almost exploded. "Hannah I am overwhelmed right now at the office. I know this is a huge, lifetime event and I promise I'll do my best to be there for Daisy... and you."

Hannah sat back and watched him. "This is pushing it, I know, but I'm going to anyway. It would be wonderful if you did something special for her on her wedding day. Got any ideas? If not, it's time to think of one."

His mind was blank, then something came to him. The stick figure picture Daisy had drawn in crayon of the two of them—a tiny girl and a big man—when she was in second grade. She had drawn a heart around the two figures. If he rushed to a local print shop and a framer, he could have a copy propped on the head table at the wedding with an inscription:

Love you with all my heart... always.

He would slip her new husband, Jack, five hundred in extra cash for the honeymoon. Guys always appreciate cash.

He smiled. "Got it covered." Then he added. "Don't look so surprised."

She wasn't smiling yet. "You have to promise me something else. You have to leave your cell phone at home on your nightstand, not only for the wedding day but starting the day before. I need you to be fully present on the day and evening of the rehearsal. Jack's parents will be in town and we're hosting them."

Dave raised his hands in surrender. "I promise."

After dinner, he took his plate to the trash can, to scrape off the few remaining scraps. He noticed down inside the can a half-crumpled note, and one word caught his attention: Yusuf. He started to bend down to recover it.

"Don't pick it up," said Hannah, standing at the sink. "I took the message when he called, then decided to toss it." She faced him, sounding irritated. "Why is he calling you at home now? What does he need that can't wait until business hours?"

Dave felt pressure in his temples. Yusuf had crashed his office just this morning, and now he was phoning here. "Am I supposed to call him back?"

"No. I lied. I told him you and I have an important engagement this evening and won't be home till late. He told me to have you call even if it's midnight. I kept my cool, but I was furious. I said, 'Whatever it is, Doctor Abdullah, it can wait.' And I hung up."

Dave nodded. What else could he tell Hannah? "You did the right thing."

"That man has no sense of boundaries or privacy. You're his accountant. He doesn't own you."

Dave slid his plate into the dishwasher, suspecting he would probably be hounded in the morning.

Chapter 2

When he walked into the office, Jen gave him an exasperated look.

"You don't even need to tell me. He called our house last evening."

"He'll call here again soon. I know it. Even though I told him you have a full schedule. Do you want to take the call, or… what do you want me to say?"

"Tell him I have someone starting the paper work. And it will take time."

"Someone? Who?"

"Mary."

"Really. Is that true?"

"No, but it will be shortly. Give me fifteen minutes to settle in, then tell her I need to see her."

*

Mary was just out of college, sharp, intense and focused—the kind of intern Dave could trust with a task that was actually a bit beyond her skillset or current level of training. She was also savvy enough to not try faking it or impress him by trying to tackle it on her own.

"This a complicated set of forms," she said, flipping through the pages. "You know, I've never handled something like this. The IRS will go through these with a fine-toothed comb."

"I know you're going to do a great job. And all I want you to do is go through them, read up on them online on the IRS website, and come back to me with a list of questions."

"Would it be possible for you to talk me through them first?"

"Truthfully, I'd have to figure them out, and that's why I'm giving you the task. I am utterly swamped with tax season work and the wedding. Just go ahead and make a list of questions. I'll oversee your work after that, don't worry."

He was passing through the outer office to get coffee, when the phone on Jen's desk rang. She pointed to caller ID.

"Guess who."

"Tell him what I told you. You won't be lying. Someone's on it."

As he walked into the kitchen, he heard Jen say, "If someone started a fund to send him away on a long trip, I'd toss in twenty bucks."

"I'd kick in fifty," he said over his shoulder.

Now that he had off-loaded the job of working on Yusuf's application for non-profit status, he could focus on getting his special gift ready for Daisy. The right-colored mat and a pretty gold frame would set off the picture nicely. The print shop three blocks away would be his next call, and he'd send Jen over with the picture.

*

The field agent in Albany looked at the bank report the IRS in DC had forwarded.

Clever, he thought, *keeping your money transfers just under ten thousand.*

Whoever Yusuf Abdullah was—if that was even his real

name—he was now on the FBI's radar.

Maybe the transfers were really going to a charitable organization. Or maybe not.

It was his job to start gathering information and finding out.

*

Jen and Cliff, her husband, slipped to the side of the crowded grand ballroom, where they caught Dave and Hannah at the punch bowl, waiting for the bridal party to arrive from post-ceremony picture-taking.

"This is some wedding crowd. Cliff and I feel like paupers."

"Stop it," said Hannah, smiling. "I'm glad you're here. Dave was just stressing about the cost of this reception at two hundred dollars per plate and an open bar. I need someone sane to talk to. Anyway, you two look like you stepped out of a fashion magazine."

Cliff laughed. "Her dress is from Off-Fifth and this is a rented tux. Look at all these other people—the glitterati, the old-money folks. I was just naming off to Jen the blue-blood, pre-Revolution families represented here. The Standishes, the Aldens, and the Bradfords. This is upper-crust, well-invested or trust-funded, conservative America in a microcosm. Anybody who's somebody is in this room."

Hannah smiled. "It just so happens; many of these people are Dave's clients and others we know through community organizations. Here come the Bradfords now."

Ginny Bradford took Hannah's hand. "So good to see you. Daisy and Jack look amazing and so happy starting their lives together."

"They are, and they're leaving from here for a dream

honeymoon in Bali."

Reggie Bradford slapped Dave on the shoulder as the women talked. "After all this hubbub, I'll bet you and Hannah could use a getaway, too."

Dave leaned close. "I am planning something. Don't say a word or it'll get back to Hannah. You know how these guys talk. I'm planning a little escape to the Middle East to see."

Cheers and clapping from the crowd interrupted him, followed by the wedding coordinator's loud announcement into the microphone.

"*Welcome the newlyweds!*"

*

As the evening wore on, Dave thought about Cliff's observation of the crowd. Personally, he could not have cared less about the status of these acquaintances, neighbors and social club cronies. Mingling with them was all part of the business. Probably the reason this crowd had showed up, and it surprised him who had accepted the invitation was the fact that he and Hannah were hosting the reception at a large, painted-lady Victorian that had been converted into a posh, event venue and there was an open bar.

"So cynical," Hannah murmured in his ear, when he confided his suspicions.

"No," he reacted. "Experienced. These people like to flash their jewelry and talk about their yachts, but just flash free drinks at them and watch them swarm like flies."

Daisy came up behind him, to whisk him onto the floor for the father-daughter dance. "Stop it. I heard that. No carping about the rich or about your clients today. After all," she waved her hand at the urns of flowers, the crystal and silver dining tables and the high-end scotch and bourbon-stocked bar. "They're paying for all this."

She was right, of course, he thought. He should be relaxed and enjoy the music, the conversations, and the food. As he clasped Daisy's hand and stepped onto the dance floor, though, he couldn't shake a small but nagging feeling.

Out on the lawn after the reception, Dave and a few of the men enjoyed scotch and cigars. An evening chill was settling in.

"I'm Scott Walters," said one of the guys, whom he'd never met before. Probably from Hannah's part of the guest list. "I'm looking to open a specialty grocery store here in Saratoga Springs. I have one in Lake Placid and one in Albany, and they're going gangbusters. Organics and locally grown produce and…"

Dave tried to focus on the conversation but found himself distracted by that uneasy feeling he couldn't identify.

"Call on Monday," he said, when the guy had asked for an appointment, "and we'll meet and get your books set up."

Late in the evening, when he and Hannah collapsed in bed, she said, "My face is sore from smiling so much. What a happy day! I just have one question?"

All he wanted to do was sink into the mattress. "What's that?"

"Where were you today?"

Dear God. Not an interrogation. Not now. One of the songs the DJ had played came to mind and he tried to distract her with his best Beach Boys impression. "Bermuda, Bahamas, c'mon, pretty Mama…"

"Don't dodge the question. I could tell when your mind was somewhere else today. What was it that's bothering you?"

He opened his mouth to say "nothing," but she would plow

right through that.

"I'm not sure," he said.

In the back of his mind, though he didn't know why, one name kept returning, troubling him.

Yusuf.

*

Mary was in his office for the second time that Tuesday morning, knocking timidly on the door and darting in to see him between his appointments.

"About this not-for-profit application form again..."

He had two minutes before the new business contact from the wedding walked in.

"Do you have all the documentation that has to go in with this form?"

"The client has to provide it all." He was surprised that Yusuf hadn't emailed everything already, since he was so anxious to get the forms submitted.

"Actually, Jen said Dr. Abdullah brought in a file with his documentation, then within an hour came and took it back. He said he needed to correct something. We're wondering if he happened to come by and hand it all to you."

That was just like a difficult client. Pressure you to get something done, but not give you the numbers or documentation you need to do your part.

"Since the entity is already functioning, there is a deadline for filing this application and it's coming up."

He was still tired from the wedding, and now he could see the grocery store guy coming in the front door.

"Call Abdullah's office and tell him to haul ass with his

documentation."

She stared.

"Of course, you don't say that. But light a fire under his butt."

Her face had fallen, and he realized he'd sounded harsh.

"Look, I'm sorry. I'm just a bit overwhelmed right now. And it's not going to get better any time soon. The truth is, I'm not going to be available to offer you a lot to help with this job. But that's why I chose you. Because you're competent. I hereby give you the authority to bug the crap out of Abdullah until you get what you need from him." He laughed at that. "Considering how much he's bugged me, turnabout is fair play."

She nodded, but looked uncertain.

"You can do this," he told her, hoping he was right. He didn't have a lot of bandwidth left to deal with a project like this.

That was not the end of it, though.

"Dr. Abdullah is just not available. He's in surgery for the next four days," Mary said a week later. "Is that even allowed? Aren't doctors supposed to space out their surgical days?"

"I would think so, but then I'm an accountant, not a hospital administrator." He realized that sounded dismissive. "How can I help you?"

"There are some questions I hope you can answer."

This was going to come back like a pesky fly you couldn't swat away.

"All right, shoot."

"Is this not-for-profit entity an outgrowth of another entity?

He rifled through his memory of the many spur-of-the-moment conversations Abdullah had pushed on him. "That would be a no."

She rapid-fired a few other questions, and he dredged up

answers from phone conversations and even from a few he'd had with Abdullah when he was caught in public and couldn't escape gracefully.

"Yes."

"No."

"Yes."

"I have a note about that somewhere. Let me find that info and get back to you."

Looking troubled, Mary tapped timidly on Dave's door again days later.

"I reached out to an accountant Dr. Abdullah tried to work with before he came to you. Not a C.P.A., just an accountant. I thought she might have some of the information needed to finish this form."

Dear Lord, can we just move this whole thing out of here. He needed Mary to focus on other projects, and this one was clearly consuming too much of her time.

"And? Was she any help?"

She bit her lower lip. "She says she was trying to verify Dr. Abdullah's information—perform an audit on it—before submitting it. She says she tried several times and got no response, and the next thing she knew, Abdullah stopped contacting her. I wonder if that's when he met you and brought his business here."

Dave ran one hand through his hair. "Yeah, and it became the gift that keeps on giving. So, the woman has none of the information we need."

"She doesn't. she suggests that whatever information we get should be audited, though."

Okay, so the doctor was a surgeon in high demand. That didn't mean he got to dump his work on someone and treat them like an underling he tagged to do his work for him.

"Getting all his information to you is the doctor's responsibility," Dave said, irritated. "If he doesn't get it to you in the next, how many days are left before the deadline?"

"Two."

"If you don't get the information from him by tomorrow, file the forms without the info the IRS wants. They'll reject his application and that'll wake him up."

One way or the other, he had to slide Dr. Abdullah off his roster of clients.

Back in her office, Mary made a note for the doctor's folder. "File form without the requested information, as per Dave's instructions."

Late the following afternoon, final numbers came in from Dr. Abdullah.

The day of the filing was due. Mary filled in the information requested, and submitted the forms at four thirty p.m., just ahead of the deadline. Fortunately, Dave's signature was not required, because he had already left for the day. No matter, Mary had the foresight to get a signature from Susan Mentor, president of Yusuf Abdullah's charitable organization.

Locking up for the evening, Mary walked home, feeling proud that on her boss's behalf, she accomplished the near impossible with a demanding and difficult client.

Chapter 3

Dr. Abdullah sounded more than moderately irritated over the phone.

"The office of my new charity has become fully operational, but we still have a problem." His voice grew intense. "A big problem."

Of course, you do, Dave grimaced. *That's what happens when you don't give people what they need to do your work.* "And that problem is—what?"

"We do not have the not-for-profit status you promised to obtain for me from the I.R.S."

The words "you promised" rankled, but Dave held back from firing the words he was thinking.

"And as a result, we cannot get the not-for-profit mailing permit we need from the U.S. Postal Service."

"We filed for that status some time ago."

"Yes, but they are not granting it."

"What's the holdup did they say?"

Yusuf muttered some criticisms about the postal service and didn't answer the question.

"What can you do to push this along?"

"I don't think you understand the IRS. You don't push them. If you do, I can guarantee they'll push back. You won't like it."

"Perhaps you should check the forms you filed. Perhaps something was not done correctly."

Dave felt a pressure behind his eyes.

"I hired you to do this because I thought you were competent to handle it."

The pressure made his head feel like it would explode, and he fought to keep the conversation on a professional, not personal, level. But it was time to turn the tables a bit.

"Doctor," he replied, "what you hired me to do is a task I've never undertaken before. I explained that several times, and you insisted you needed my help. I've given it to the best of my ability."

"You told me you were 'happy to assist my cause'—those were your words. I remember distinctly."

Dave hated having his own words flung back in his face.

Do you remember telling me you'd give us everything we needed and asked for?

"Imagine you're in the middle of an operation, and you turn to your surgical staff and ask for something or an implement you need and they don't give it to you."

"What are you saying? That the delay has something to do with me? I sent you to the right people, who should have had the information you needed. I'm a busy man, and I rely on my support people. After all, you're professionals, too."

This guy was skilled at turning the blame for non-performance and incompetence onto other people.

"Those people did not give us what we needed. And when my intern tried to get information from you."

"The oversight of an intern is your responsibility, is it not? She is just like a... like a secretary, correct? You filled out the forms, did you not?"

Dave fumbled at this. He hadn't filled them out. He had let Mary carry the ball. Maybe he should have checked himself and his own urge to get Yusuf off his back.

"We filed right at the deadline—or you would have had to wait a long time to refile—and we did so with the information provided to us."

"Why was I not told the deadline was approaching so quickly?"

Had Mary passed along that important piece of information?

"You know my organization's work is important, do you not?"

He was feeling pinned to the wall, and hated that feeling. How did he even get into this mess?

So much for trying to be a good guy.

"All my clients are important. And yes, I know your work is important."

"Do you not feel the urgency—the fact that people right now are homeless and starving without our help?"

Dave could see the tears in Yusuf's eyes. "Yes, I support what you're doing—"

Yusuf started to say something more, but this time Dave interrupted.

"I know the urgency you're feeling. But I'm not comfortable with some of the things your organization is doing. You've pushed ahead without proper authorization."

Yusuf was silent for a brief moment, and wiped his eyes with the back of one hand. When he spoke again, his voice was choked with emotion.

"People in my homeland are dying. You took weeks and weeks to drag out the process of filing the right government forms. Do you think I should have waited around, twiddling my thumbs, while bureaucrats who do nothing but scan computer files and rubber stamp pieces of paper take their sweet time giving us approval?

"You knew the urgency of this matter." His voice rose a little. "You said you believe in and support our cause."

Dave needed to calm this conversation down. Get it off the emotional, slightly accusatory track it was sliding down and back up on an even professional footing.

"The proper form has been filed." But had it been done correctly? Completely? A sudden stab of professional conscience hit its mark.

"And now I have to wait?" Yusuf pressed. "That's it?"

Dave could imagine more delays on the part of the IRS and the postal service. More agitated phone calls from Yusuf.

"I'll make a call and see if there is anything I can do to urge this along."

The I.R.S. agent on the phone was anything but helpful.

"You realize, of course, that your submission came in just before the deadline. The time stamp says you got it in at the 'eleventh hour.' If there was some urgency about this, it's not reflected in the manner in which this was handled."

He didn't want to sound unprofessional and like he was blaming the client. I was, after all, his firm that had submitted the application.

"We supplied you with the information we thought was needed to get results for our client."

"With so much important information left out?"

That came like a kick in the groin.

"We didn't want to miss the submission deadline."

"But this organization was raising and transferring funds for months before this application came to us."

That made him hesitate for a second. How did this agent know that? He settled on the fact that this *was* the all-seeing I.R.S., after all. What didn't they know? Maybe not the color of his underwear, but security surveillance had spiked after 9/11. *So maybe they know that, too.*

He refrained from saying anything sarcastic.

"And you signed off on this form in its current state," the agent continued. "Is that correct?"

"Yes."

"You are aware the information is quite incomplete. I'd like to ask, what were you expecting, in terms of a response from the Internal Revenue Service?"

Dave felt pressure coming at him from both sides: the I.R.S. and, most definitely from Yusuf, if he didn't help the guy get his organization up and running legitimately.

Don't push. Don't be rude. And don't say you were expecting them to push back on the client for the necessary information—how unprofessional do you want to sound?

"Look, I only called to check on the status and see if anything can be done to move this application along."

When the conversation ended, the IRS agent showed the notes he'd carefully taken to his supervisor, then as instructed, typed them into an email to the FBI and hit *Send*.

*

A week later, on the way into the office, Dave noticed that the gutters needed to be cleaned out. One was sagging and if it wasn't attended to, it could tear away. The landscaper hadn't shown up either, which meant he'd have to come back one evening and trim the hedges himself.

What was that saying about good help being hard to come by?

"You're going to need an aspirin," Jen said, handing him the phone message.

Dave read it, looked at the time Jen had written and underlined—*8.37 a.m.*—and blew out a long breath.

"I can't even get into the office and he's already calling. One of these days he'll be waiting for me on the sidewalk."

Jen shook her head. "Don't even say that or you'll make it real."

"Do we have any aspirin?"

"Ibuprofen. In the cabinet above the kitchen sink."

*

It took all morning to get to the right supervisor at the main post office in Albany to return his call. And it was late in the afternoon when the man got back to him. Between the contacts, the guy's tone of voice changed, from helpful sounding to—what was it? —annoyed? wary?

"I looked up your client's complaint and his file. His organization submitted a request to be granted postage-free status as a non-profit some months ago, that's true."

Dave knew what was coming next, and rubbed his temple.

"But there's no indication they were granted I.R.S. status as a non-profit. The notes show that his organization has called us several times, and the last postal agent's notes say they were pretty *demanding*. You, as a professional, should know that doesn't score points or get you the status you need."

Dave was quick to distance himself. "Sir, I did not know about these previous calls."

"If that's the case, perhaps you should check with your client before calling us."

"I guess there's no way to give them some kind of

provisional non-profit status. Like 'status pending'?"

"None. And can I give you a word to the wise?—There's no point in pushing."

Dave backed off. He wasn't about to explain how he was being pushed. Why would this guy care? And it was clear that pleading his own case—his desire to get his client off his back—wouldn't help anyway.

When he hung up, he knew his next step, and dreaded it.

*

Yusuf's voice on the phone was level and patient. That was something of a relief.

"You are a good man," he said. "A very good man. I can't thank you enough. God will bless you for all your efforts on our behalf."

Actually, the change in tone threw Dave off completely. He was intending to come down hard on Yusuf about pressuring him, but there was no way after the doctor's next words.

"I pray for you and your wife and daughter every day, Dave. Every day."

Impossible to throw a verbal punch now.

"Please, Yusuf. Have your people assemble all the information needed by the IRS. That's the bottleneck preventing everything else from happening for your organization. You won't be granted official status without it."

Yusuf's voice remained calm, but his old line of rhetoric was the same. "And in the meantime, my poor people…"

Get off your ass and get the right information to the U.S. Government, if you care so much.

Dave had a sobering thought.

"You're not soliciting funds by mail, are you? And if so, you're not indicating that those funds can be considered a charitable donation, are you?"

"David, I have given over one million dollars of my own money to this work."

That didn't answer the questions.

"What about soliciting funds?"

"Many people are eager to help with the cause. They're at work behind the scenes already."

Another dodge.

"Look," Dave said, "you can't be doing what it sounds like you're doing. The IRS will shut you down permanently if you don't stop; you definitely can't involve me."

"My people..."

Like trying to blast through granite. Was Yusuf this thick-headed? Not possible. He was a highly trained and skilled surgeon. His determination was clearly blinding him.

"Let me just say one thing—and this comes from the fact that I don't know how things are done in your country, so don't take it the wrong way." He suspected he did know—that pressure and pay-offs worked there.

"But you can't do things the way you're trying to do them here. You could wind up in some trouble, or at least pay some hefty fines."

Yusuf was conciliatory. "You are a good friend, Dave. You are watching my back. I always knew you would be on my side."

Time to clear this call. Other deadline work was going to take up this day.

"I am totally on your side in this matter. That's why I'm trying to shield you from problems with the government."

The recording of this conversation would be edited to reflect select statements.

Yusuf's assertions: "I have given over a million dollars of my own money..." and "Many people are eager to help with the cause. They're at work behind the scenes already."

And Dave's last words: "I am totally on your side..." and "I'm trying to shield you from problems with the government."

*

He dropped his briefcase by the front door and followed the sound of TV news into the kitchen, where Hannah was staring at the screen. A box of ribs and sides sat on the table. Supper.

"More civilians killed in Iraq," she said, nodding at the images of collapsed buildings, twisted metal, and the bodies of children lying in rubble. "So, upsetting. Those poor people. They wanted Saddam gone, but they didn't expect to be slaughtered in the process."

"My poor people."

He was hoping to escape all pressure and responsibility this evening, most especially Yusuf's fervent attempts to make him feel guilty for not walking face-first into it over dinner.

"Can we turn that off?"

Hannah turned to him, frowning.

"Dave, it's a humanitarian disaster. Imagine if that was us. Or our daughter and son-in-law. Our grandbabies. The least we can do is keep up with what's happening to them over there. Stay informed."

A young woman was holding a limp, bloodied child on her lap, rocking and wailing. The child's head lolled, as if it were dead or unconscious.

"Oh, I'm not uninformed, trust me."

"Yusuf?—still coming down on you?"

"Like a truckload of cinderblocks."

The reporter was saying, over the images of makeshift hospital cots filled with bandaged bombing victims, "The need for relief in the form of medical supplies and food is intense. The level of suffering is off the scale."

Hannah turned off the TV.

"You're right, I guess. You can only take seeing so much of this. I'll get some plates; you get the forks and napkins."

Right. A dose of suffering and barbecue sauce. Perfect.

At the end of dinner, Hannah seemed to be lost in serious thought.

"Are you still thinking about the news?" Dave asked.

"I want to make a donation. I heard that our church is mounting an effort. Are you okay with that?"

He nodded. "Of course, I am."

For the rest of the evening, he unloaded a few files from his briefcase and then went outside to water the gardens. He could not get the terrible images from Iraq out of his head.

Chapter 4

Jen had a curious look when she poked her head into Dave's office door.

"It's the U.S. Postal Service calling from Albany."

"Why are they calling me?" Yusuf had assured him someone in his organization would take care of the I.R.S. issue.

"Do you want me to ask?"

"No. I'll take it. Which line are they on?"

"The one that's blinking impatiently."

The supervisor who was calling had the same questions he had asked Dave weeks before when he had called Albany to check on Yusuf's non-profit postal waiver.

"Did you fill out this application?"

"No. My client did."

"Why is your phone number listed on it?"

"I didn't know it was."

There was a long pause. Dave thought he heard a series of clicks.

"*Hello?*" He didn't have time to go over the same ground again with the postal service. With any luck, they had disconnected, and he wouldn't be available if they called back.

"You say you didn't know your phone number was listed on the application."

"Yes, that is what I said."

"Are you an official with this organization?"

"No. I'm Dr. Abdullah's accountant."

"You have no other official capacity with his organization."

This guy is dumb or stupid or both.

"None. I just told you."

Another, longer pause.

"Are you aware he is soliciting funds via the U.S. Postal Service, and that his mailings insinuate those donations are tax-exempt? Our notes say that his organization has not been granted that status yet."

Sonofa... Dave sat up in his chair, pissed at Yusuf and fighting to keep his cool. Another thought occurred. *If the post office and the I.R.S. are looking into this, be careful what you say next.*

"You said in a previous conversation that you support Dr. Abdullah's work completely."

"I do, but..."

"And you're his accountant, helping him to set up his charity. But you're denying that you have any knowledge about his financial solicitations."

He started to lose it and irritation crept into his voice. "Yes, I am his accountant. But, *as I said*, I have no knowledge of his day-to-day operations or his solicitations."

"But if money comes into his organization, surely you see those deposits."

A ton more cinder blocks fell.

If money was coming in, where was it being deposited? He hadn't seen anything irregular in the statements Yusuf's assistant dropped off to be entered into the accounting ledgers.

"Mr. Mattson?"

He felt somewhere between stupid and angry, and a little like an animal suddenly wary of being trapped.

Still, honesty was always the best policy.

"I do see all Dr. Abdullah's bank deposits. Generally speaking. But I have to ask, if you're with the postal service, why are you asking financially oriented questions?"

"You see his bank deposits 'generally speaking.'"

All at once, something seemed way off. Was this a simple request for information, or an interrogation?

"I'm sorry," he said quickly, "but I'm looking at the clock in my office and I see that I'm very late for an important appointment. You'll have to direct your questions to Dr. Abdullah's organization. I'm sure you have their number."

The last statement sounded sarcastic, and when he hung up, he wished it hadn't hung up or sounded sarcastic. That was not his professional style, regardless of who he was talking to or how annoying they were.

For the rest of the day, though, a question stuck with him. Who had he been talking to?

*

On the way home that day, he made a stop he'd been meaning to make for a week or so.

"Evelyn, how's my girlfriend?" Dave said.

Evelyn looked around the sitting room of the nursing facility, hoping someone would hear her reply. "For five dollars, I'd take all my clothes off and streak the town."

Dave smiled. "People would talk."

"If they're not talking about you, you're doing something wrong. What's in the brown paper bag? You didn't lift that off some bum, did you?" She laughed.

He pulled a bottle from the bag. Glenfiddich, twenty years old. "Not hardly."

She eyed him. "You sound fine, but you look stressed—again. You're months past Daisy's wedding, so what's troubling you now?"

He didn't want to burden her with details of a mess she had nothing to do with and she couldn't do a thing about it. A headline would do.

"The Government."

She held out a glass, and when he poured her a finger of scotch, she shook it a little. "What are you saving it for? Christmas? I might not be here. You can be a little more generous with that stuff."

He laughed. "You're going to outlive me."

She savored the first sip. And the second and third.

"Don't trust them for half a minute," she said, finally.

Dave let the burn of the drink subside.

"Who are we talking about? The Government?"

"They destroyed my father and uncle during the McCarthy era."

Dave set his glass down. "That's terrible. You never said anything about that. How?"

"My family was made to feel ashamed. They had done nothing wrong, but it was drilled into us not to speak of it. You know how people are. Where there's smoke."

"What happened?—if you don't mind talking about it now."

"No, I don't mind. Everyone's dead but me. McCarthy lost his damn mind and saw Communists everywhere. You do know that people lost their careers, their homes and their friends. Some committed suicide. All because the government wanted to see what they wanted to see. If someone asked for Russian dressing on their salad, they were a Communist. It was insanity."

"And your father and uncle?"

"They had an import business in New York, and the man who brokered their deals in Europe was a Russian man. It didn't matter that he was Jewish and his family had escaped Russia to live in England. He came to the U.S. to visit with my father and uncle for business reasons, and someone reported that they were 'dealing with the Russians.' They were followed down the streets of New York and in the subways by government goons. You see, in the midst of the McCarthy madness, that's all it took. Someone reported something that wasn't even true, but you were implicated."

For a moment, her eyes clouded and her lips trembled. But it was clear she was determined not to cry.

Dave nodded. "That's terrible."

He had heard, of course, that things like she was describing had happened, but he'd never heard it from someone he knew personally. Listening to Evelyn, watching her fight back the remembered sadness, he felt the helplessness and horror of it.

He laid one hand on her forearm.

"So sorry, Ev."

She took another sip of scotch. Then a long, deep breath.

"In the end, McCarthy got his, that bastard. But not before thousands and thousands of lives were ruined."

"Damn shame," Dave said. "Something like that could happen in America, where you're supposed to be innocent until proven guilty."

"Ha!" she scoffed. "If the government says you're guilty, you might as well kiss your freedom goodbye."

All the way home, he wished he'd had a second shot of scotch. Or a double.

*

"So, there it is. He admits to seeing Abdullah's bank deposits."

The U.S. Attorney, sat back in his chair and loosened his tie a little more. "I can't go anywhere with this. Abdullah's office help may see them, too. Doesn't mean anything."

"It's a link."

"A first link—maybe. You F.B.I. guys need to do what you're paid to do."

"We've got him on a recording, saying he sees the statements. Then he sounds nervous, makes up a bullshit lie, and hangs up. Makes it sound like he's hiding something. That characterizes him as hiding something."

The attorney shook his head. "Get your thumb out, and bring me more."

"You guys at the DOJ are a pain in the ass. 'Bring us a needle in a haystack.' 'Bring us anything.' You keep pushing us so you can put together a case."

"You don't want to go on record as saying that, do you? You know the order that's come down."

Silence.

The attorney pointed to newspapers he had framed and hung on his office wall.

The New York Times
U.S. ATTACKED
HIJACKED JETS DESTROY TWIN TOWERS
AND HIT PENTAGON IN DAY OF TERROR

The Washington Times
INFAMY

"Do your goddam job. We need our own body count. Bring me what I need, whatever it takes. When we're done, I need something that's going to squeeze his balls till he sings like a fat lady at the opera."

*

Hannah's request for Spanish saffron meant cutting his lunch break short and driving to the specialty grocer.

How the hell was he supposed to find an exotic spice, when he had no clue what it was and the young woman whom he asked for help looked confused. "Is that a kind of fish?"

"I can show you where it is," said a familiar voice behind him.

Steve Bantry, manager of his local bank, was behind him, pointing down an aisle. "I'm here for something else, but my wife cooks with it."

Halfway down the aisle, Bantry stopped and looked both ways, checking to be sure no one was within earshot. He had a look of grave concern.

"Look, Dave, I could lose my job for telling you this, but you're a good guy, one of the most honest businessmen in town, so I think you deserve to know." He looked up and down the aisle again.

"Know what?"

Bantry eyed him before answering. "What do you know about Yusuf Abdullah? I mean, how closely do you have your hand on the pulse of his organizations?"

"I see the books that are delivered to my office."

"That's it? You don't have any more detail than that about his finances. I thought you would, being his accountant."

Dave felt his face redden. Normally, he would dig in more, ask for details to support records.

Bantry looked at him closely, as if he were watching for a reaction.

"Abdullah has been transferring money from several banks to Iraq. He's under investigation by the IRS. Probably other agencies too. Are you sure you don't know anything more about him and his financial dealings?"

Dave's throat felt dry. "I don't." The answer sounded bad.

"You've got to promise me you won't tell anyone I told you this. Anyone. I'd be out on the street in a heartbeat and I doubt any other bank would ever hire me. If I were you, I'd shore up my defenses because an earthquake could be headed your way."

*

Lying in bed, Dave tossed and turned in the dark.

Hannah switched her bedside lamp on low.

"What's going on, Dave? You're coming out of your skin; I can feel it."

"It's nothing. Go back to sleep."

She sat up, and turned the light up brighter. "Don't lie to me. I'm not a child you have to protect. What is it?"

"I don't want you to worry."

"You think I haven't been concerned for the last couple of weeks? You're pacing. You're hardly eating. You pay less attention when I talk than you usually do. Is it another woman? Cancer? *What?*"

He blew out a long breath, and sat up. Reaching across the covers, he took her hand.

"I can't believe you'd think—"

"Just tell me. You're driving me nuts."

"It's Abdullah."

"I told you weeks ago to drop him like a snake."

"Not him exactly. I got a call about him. The whole thing felt weird, and I think it was recorded."

"By who? What was it about?"

He quickly related the details of the call.

"I had the sense the whole time that someone else was listening besides the postal inspector. There was a kind of hollow sound on the line and I kept hearing clicks. I didn't think anything of it until, well, there was a moment when the guy's voice sounded on edge and the mood changed."

"What did you tell them? You can't be in any trouble. It's Abdullah's organization that dropped the ball with the application."

"It wasn't that. They wanted to know if I saw his bank deposit statements, and I said, 'generally, yes.'"

She waited. "So…?"

"So, if he is doing something shady, soliciting funds illegally, that implicates me."

"Oh, Dave. Did you see anything wrong with the statements?"

"That's just it. I've been so busy with everything, really under the gun, I didn't…" He broke off.

Hannah waited. "You didn't really review them carefully, did you?"

"I could kick myself in the ass."

"You don't have to. I'll do it. After all these years in business, with a great reputation *and* with Abdullah as demanding and unhelpful as he is, how could you get slack when it comes to *his* financial affairs?"

He ran his hands through his hair.

"You're not helping."

"Let's just hope you're just overworked and being paranoid about this. And dump Abdullah. You don't need to go to prison or lose all your clients because of some pushy clown."

When she turned off the light, he rolled over and punched his pillow.

That's the best I can hope for—that I'm just being paranoid? Forget the possible felony charge.

Long after Hannah's breathing had slipped into the long, slow rhythm that told him she was asleep, he stared at the dark ceiling.

Just exactly whose desk was the application sitting on? The one he had neglected to review but signed off on.

*

Hannah was subdued when he walked into the kitchen. His favorite breakfast eggs over easy, bacon, and toast with orange marmalade—were on the table.

"Peace offering," she said, when he looked at her questioningly. "I shouldn't help boost your cholesterol, but I was too rough on you last night."

He hugged her and kissed her cheek. "So, a makeup breakfast. How about makeup sex instead?"

She pushed him away, smiling. "You're incorrigible."

"That's one of my finer traits."

"It's getting cold. Eat."

Halfway through breakfast, when he was on his second cup of coffee, he said, "I think I was a bit paranoid. It didn't help that I stopped to see Evelyn, and she told me about her father being ruined during the McCarthy, Communist witch hunts."

"Dear Evelyn. I'm sure that left a terrible scar on her. But, Dave, that was decades ago. Eighty years. That kind of thing could never happen again in this country. There have to be some kind of safeguards, right?"

When he set his dishes in the dishwasher, Hannah was standing there with the dog leash.

"I'll be late," he protested.

"*You* need to slow down. And the dog needs to poo. There was an unpleasant surprise on the carpet yesterday."

He looked at the shih-tzu.

"If you weren't so cute, I'd have you stuffed."

"*Dave.*"

*

Why do I let myself in for this? he thought, watching the shih-tzu sniff at every lamppost, street sign, and stalk of grass for several blocks, without doing what he was supposed to do.

He glanced at his watch, and happened to catch sight of a brown Ford sedan.

Wasn't that there on our block when we set out?

The dog yipped at a small bird that was pecking for worms in the grass strip along the curb.

"*Go already,*" he said, giving the leash a gentle tug. "I've got to get to work to keep you in kibbles and silly dog sweaters."

When they came to the next intersection in the neighborhood, where they usually went straight, heading for the park, a thought occurred to him and he quickly turned down the side street instead.

A dozen yards down that street, he looked back.

No brown Ford sedan.

Sorry about what happened all those years ago, Ev, but you messed with my head.

Just before the next intersection, the shih-tzu finally decided it was time and squatted.

I love you, too, buddy, Dave thought, *but now I've got to carry your mess home in this little plastic bag. You owe me bigtime.*

When the dog was done, he decided not to turn around and return to their street to go directly home but to circle around on the back street. The morning air was fresh, and yeah, he needed to slow down.

Turning off the side street they'd been on, he didn't see when a brown Ford sedan turned onto it, carefully following at a distance.

Chapter 5

Jen set a stack of letters on his desk, but didn't charge out as usual.

"Something I need to know?" Dave said, looking away from his computer. "It's not the gutters again, is it? I paid a lot to get them fixed."

"I haven't wanted to bother you with this."

"*But…*"

"It's silly."

"Jen, I've got to finish these emails, then review that stack of returns you just brought me."

She was working her hands nervously, uncharacteristically.

"It's silly because it's broad daylight and it's happening totally out in the open. There's this car that I've seen parked down the street every day for almost two weeks. The same car. And there are two guys in the front seat, just sitting there, watching."

Dave felt a wave of cold go through him.

Jen went on. "And I swear this is the part that makes me sound like an overwrought female, I know—I swear they're watching the office."

Did he really want to know?

"By any chance, is it a brown Ford sedan?"

"Yes. Have you noticed it, too? I mentioned it to Mary, and she said there's two men in suits inside."

He wanted to make a joke. "They're either Mormons or

Fuller Brush salesmen," but his sense of humor was dissolving fast.

"Maybe we should report it to the police. Let them check it out."

"That's the thing. I did report it after a few days. Mary was really nervous about walking outside. I didn't hear anything back from the police, so I called and talked to a superior officer. He said, and I quote, 'There's no vehicle matching that description parked on your street.'

"Dave, I was looking out the front door while I was talking to him and the car was right there. So, what was that about?"

Dave pushed back from his desk. "Is the car there now?"

"It was when I came in here. I just looked."

*

Dave could feel his heartbeat as he strode down the sidewalk. Down in the next block, a few hundred feet away, was the brown Ford sedan. Even with the glare of daylight on the windshield, he could make out two figures in the front seat.

Crossing the street to the side the vehicle was parked on, his mind returned to the phone conversation with the postal inspector. This couldn't possibly be related. Was it absurd to think he was being surveilled? For what reason? Surely, if someone needed to ask him questions, they would just knock on his door and ask.

Before he reached the other sidewalk, he heard the sound of a car engine starting and paused to stare.

Down the street, the sedan pulled out quickly and made a sharp U-turn, tires squealing.

Without thinking, he charged out into the street and sprinted after it.

What do you think you're going to see? Maybe a government license plate.

What he got was only a glimpse before the vehicle made a fast right turn at the next corner and was gone.

*

Jen looked over his shoulder as they peered at Dave's computer screen.

"Are you sure?"

Dave tapped the screen. "Positive. I didn't get the plate number, but I'm sure that it was a Maryland tag."

Why would a car with those plates be parked on our street every day with two guys watching the office?" Then she tried to shake it off. "We have to be mistaken. There's no reason for anyone to be watching this office. My God, we're a small, hometown-based accounting business. Maybe they're commercial real estate brokers."

He pressed his lips together, wishing she was right but feeling more certain now that the phone interrogation had been about more than just an application with the post office.

*

"Lawyer up," said Evelyn loudly, slapping a blue-veined hand on the arm of her chair.

There was the fire Dave loved to see in her, but not in relation to these events.

"I don't have any reason to lawyer up," he responded.

"You asked me what would I do, and I'm telling you. Don't

be stubborn. My father said over and over that he had nothing to hide and it didn't matter."

"Do you still have that bottle of Glenfiddich?"

"I'm not a lush. Of course, I do. But all I've got to drink it out of is little, plastic pill cups they bring three times a damn day."

"That'll work, unless you just want to swig and pass it."

When she returned with the bottle and cups, she asked, "What does Hannah say?"

"I'm not going to tell her about the sedan yet."

"Why the hell not? Why do you men always think you have to shield us from difficult things? Then later, you kick yourself for not taking our advice."

"I think I just need to take some time off. Let whatever's going on blow over."

She huffed at that. "In other words, ignore it and it'll go away. That's how small lumps turn into untreatable cancers."

He was feeling a little irritated at her pushing, but also knew there was a chance—a small chance—she might be right. What if this was something that wouldn't just go away?

She backed off, but only a little. "The last few times you've been here, you've looked exhausted. Like an overworked plow horse."

He poured them each a small shot of scotch.

"Look," he said, "I don't even know for sure that something *is* going on. Don't get mad at me for saying this, but I think you and Hannah pushed my anxiety buttons."

"And the fact that the police said there was no car of that description on your street—and there was. And they pulled out when they saw you coming. What about that?"

"I don't make mountains out of mole hills. Jen changed her

mind and said, she thinks they might have been real estate guys."

Evelyn shook her head, and had a frustrated look. "Men. You always think you know best, you make light of things, and then the ground falls out beneath your feet."

Maybe we just don't like to make a big deal out of things.

He raised his little, plastic shot glass. "Here's to us men."

*

Four evenings later, the phone rang just before dark and Hannah answered it.

When she hung up, she came into the family room, looking pale and upset.

"That was Carolyn, our neighbor, four doors down."

Dave looked up from the baseball game. "And?"

"She was out for an evening jog, and a car she was passing rolled down the window and stopped her to ask questions about us."

He picked up the remote and turned down the volume. "What did they want to know?"

"How well does she know us? Does she see a certain car parked at our house a lot?"

"What car?"

"They showed her a picture of a silver Mercedes."

Doctor Abdullah's car.

"What did she tell them?"

"She said she only knows us casually, that we're not close friends. And she told them she's not in the habit of watching any of her neighbors and has no clue who comes and goes at whose house. That's it's none of her business."

"How many men in the car?"

"Two. In suits."

"Did she say what kind of car they were driving?"

"Brown, with Maryland plates. Dave, what's going on?"

He turned off the TV, all interest in the game gone.

I wish I knew.

*

Dr. Janelle Harcourt unfolded her menu, the broad blue expanse of Lake George behind her on the restaurant's veranda.

"Dr. Abdullah said you're the man to handle our accounting business. Thanks for meeting me for lunch."

Dave was only too happy to be picking up a successful radiology business as a client, even if the reference to Abdullah sounded a flat note.

"Do you work with Abdullah a lot?" he said, making conversation.

"Not closely. His patients come through. That's all. Frankly…" she stopped herself from saying whatever she was about to say.

He raised his eyebrows in question.

"Frankly, he keeps hitting me up for a donation to his cause, but I'm expanding my practice and the investment I need to make is huge. More office space, new equipment, and more supplies. I hate to sound like I don't care about humanitarian emergencies, but, well, I'll have to help out another time."

He scanned the menu. *Expensive*. Huge business investment or not, she wasn't stinting herself on lunch.

She wasn't quite finished with her thoughts about Abdullah. "On the other hand, he can be."

"A bit too forceful?" he supplied.

"That, yes."

She folded her menu. "But I know his heart is in the right place. Everyone in the medical field around this region loves him. They think he's a saint. Even if he is a bit of a..." Again, she stopped herself.

Pain in the ass? Is that the word you're looking for? He settled for another term.

"High-pressure salesman?"

"I know his work overseas is urgent. I can forgive him for pushing a bit too hard. He's a good soul and a top-flight surgeon."

Once again, Dave thought that, despite his annoying side, that was the general consensus. A good man with a desperate cause.

When the wait person arrived, he relaxed and ordered the braised lamb, his favorite. On a beautiful day like this, with new business coming in and a perfectly shimmering lake view, why not relax after a couple weeks of feeling unsettled?

And anyway, if there was something going on with Dr. Abdullah, it sure had nothing to do with him.

*

"Can you tell me why these guys are in town and who they're watching?" the patrolman asked.

"Way above your pay grade and mine," the supervisor replied.

"My patrol partner Jim, and I are wondering if it has to do with this war on terror. I mean, if there's a terrorist cell here in Saratoga, shouldn't we know about it?"

"Let me put it to you in dollars and cents. My brother-in-law works at the Department of Justice in DC, and he told me on the quiet that the government is planning to share about a trillion dollars each with the Departments of Defense and Homeland Security. A trillion *each.* They don't need street cops getting in the way of their show."

The patrolman nodded. "So, you're saying this is a *federalista* show. With that kind of money being spread around, no wonder they don't want us in on the action."

"I'm not saying anything. Stop asking questions and get yourself over to the Saratoga Performing Arts Center. Bon Jovi is playing tonight and the women are going to go berserk, trying to climb on stage."

"So that's it. Something really big may finally be going down in this town, and all we get to do is tackle drunken Bon Jovi fans."

"Could be a lot worse. Could be some old, sixties band like the Beach Boys. Last year, we arrested a couple of feisty old women with walkers."

When the patrolman was gone, the supervisor pushed back in his chair, remembering the phone call.

"Stand down. Stay away from this. This is top security clearance only."

*

When they pulled into the parking lot at the mountain resort deep in the Catskills, Dave was trying not to be irritated about the fast one Hannah had pulled.

"Wait, you did what?" he had barked, discovering her folding things into the two suitcases.

"I had Jen cancel your appointments for tomorrow, and we're taking off for the weekend."

"I can't believe you would do that behind my back," Dave said, grousing.

"Jen rescheduled everyone for next week. Don't worry, Mr. Workaholic; it will be waiting for you when you get back. I knew this was the only way to drag you out of town on a Friday for a long weekend getaway. And—you'll love this, Mr. Pinchpenny—I found a place that offers a three-day package at thirty percent off because it's shoulder season and they're hungry for tourists."

Her determined expression and hands on hips made him laugh a little. "So, who am I—Mr. Workaholic or Mr. Pinchpenny? I'm confused."

"Both." She laughed.

*

From the front desk of the mountain resort, the manager greeted them as they dragged suitcases across the lobby.

"Mr. and Mrs. Mattson, welcome." He smiled broadly. "I hope you had a pleasant drive."

Hannah dug in her purse for the printed confirmation.

Dave pulled out his wallet, to hand over a credit card for the resort to keep on file, when a thought occurred.

"How did you know who we were before we told you?"

The manager's broad smile remained, but the light in it changed subtly, and he hesitated slightly before answering.

"Your wife gave us an approximate arrival time."

Hannah had produced the confirmation number, as another couple was shlepping luggage in through the lobby doors.

Dave felt a nagging sense of wariness.

"Then I guess you know these people, too. Let's see how

good you are. Try for two in a row? If you get it, I'll buy you a beer later."

The manager's face reddened a little, and he ignored that, turning his attention to Hannah.

"Here are your room keys." He rang a bell and a bellhop appeared with a cart. "Please show the Mattsons to their room."

"What was that all about?" Hannah said, when they were alone in their room.

"It struck me as odd, that's all."

"You're not on-duty, detective Mattson."

"Pretty soon, I won't know who I am."

"LIGH-TEN UP," Hannah said. "Look, I'm going to take a twenty-minute power nap, and then we're going out on the walking trails. There's a great view of the Hudson Valley from up here."

*

"I can't believe you didn't pack my camera," Dave said, as they stepped out on an overlook after an hour's leisurely walk on rocky, winding, forested trails.

The broad ribbon of the Hudson River lay in the steep valley that spread north and south far below them.

"I'm not your mother. If you weren't so busy making business calls right up until bedtime *and* before we left home this morning, you might have remembered it yourself. You're not going to be this way the whole weekend, are you?"

A hawk circled in the expanse of open air out over the river, and a warm breeze brought the scent of pine and balsam.

In the back of his mind, something felt off.

Let it all go; he coached himself. *Hannah went through a lot of trouble to make this weekend happen.*

He reached out and squeezed her hand. "You're the best. You're too good to me."

"Don't I know it. My mother always said so too."

*

An hour later, coming off the trail at the end of the resort's parking lot, Hannah was saying, "I booked us for a massage tomorrow, and…"

Dave froze in his tracks, staring across the lot. At the far end, half-concealed by the hotel's van, was a brown Ford sedan.

"Oh. My. God," the words came out.

Hannah laughed. "You sound upset. Are you worried about a massage therapist putting their hands on you? They don't care that you're out of shape and lumpy."

He hadn't taken his eyes off the car, and an unsettling thought slammed him in the head—the reason the manager knew who they were before they said their names.

They must have shown the hotel a picture. Which means they also knew we were going to be here this weekend. Did the hotel tip them off when we arrived?

Now, Hannah saw the car too.

Before Dave could stop her, she began charging across the blacktop.

"This car has been parked just down the street from our house for days. *I've had it.*"

"Why didn't you tell me?" Dave said, charging after her, reaching for her arm to stop her, but she pulled it away from him.

Before they reached the sedan, they could see there was no one in it. What they also saw was the camera with a telephoto lens sitting on the dashboard and aimed at the hotel entrance. The car had a Maryland license plate.

"That camera is blinking," Hannah said, agitated.

"That means it's recording."

"This is the same car that's been parked in our neighborhood. I didn't want to go near it, but Carolyn jogged past it again and told me there was a camera on its dashboard, pointed at our house. *Who are these people? Are they spying on us?*"

"I don't know. But I don't want to stand out here at the lonely end of a parking lot and find out."

*

"Why didn't you tell me Carolyn kept seeing that car in our neighborhood or about the camera?"

"Because I wanted to get you out of town and away for the weekend and I knew you wouldn't leave home if I told you. We needed this break."

Dave stepped over the window and looked out from just behind the curtain. It crossed his mind to tell Evelyn that men weren't the only ones to withhold information.

The car was gone.

And the next morning, with their weekend wrecked and after no sleep, they drove the three hours home in a tense silence.

Near home, the gas gauge almost on E. Dave pulled into a station to fill up. Hannah was upset enough and didn't need to find the tank empty in the morning.

Running his card at the pump, he heard someone call his name.

Ron, somebody from the gym, called over to him from the next set of pumps.

"Haven't seen you in a while. You should come back and work out. They've got new equipment. And hey"—he patted his gut— "at our age, we can all use it."

Dave forced a smile and a "Right. How ya doin,' Ron?"

"Could be better, honestly. My wife quit her job this week. Her boss, who's been a really nice guy all along, apparently went nuts all of a sudden, making the whole office tense and everyone miserable. When he shouted at her in front of everyone for the third time, she said, 'That's it.' Can't blame her really, but that kicks a big hole in our income."

Dave had finished filling up. "Bosses can be jerks. I know. I am one."

As they pulled into the driveway, the memory of a conversation at the gym maybe a year ago hit him like a lightning strike. Ron had mentioned the name of his wife's employer.

"He's a big deal, heart surgeon Dr. Abdullah."

Hannah reached for the door handle but stopped. "What is it?"

"Maybe nothing."

"Stop doing that. Tell me."

"As long as you stop withholding information from me, too."

"Tell me."

"I think something big and not very good is going on with Yusuf Abdullah."

She took a long breath and held it.

Dave faced her. "Thank you for not saying, 'I told you so.'"

She let out a breath. "You're welcome. But, for the record."

Chapter 6

"It was your men who tipped our hand over the weekend."

"You're moving too slowly. I needed to push things along."

"Why? Investigations take time."

The U.S. Attorney pointed to a collection of pictures of official mugshots on his wall. "Do you see these guys? You know who they are, correct? Or I'm assuming you do, if you're bothering to keep up."

The agent ignored the insult and glanced at the gallery of perpetrators' photos.

There was John Walker Lindh, sentenced to twenty years in prison for conspiring with the Taliban to kill U.S. citizens.

Richard Colvin Reid, in prison for life for attempting to bomb a transcontinental flight using a shoe bomb.

There was a row of pictures, of the men known as the Lackawanna Six, a U.S. terror cell, who had received prison terms ranging from seven to ten years for providing material support or resources to al-Qaeda.

Another line of photos were members of a Portland terrorist cell, sentenced to prison terms of three to eighteen years for plotting to provide assistance to the Taliban in fighting against U.S. troops in Afghanistan.

"I am familiar with all these cases, of course. The FBI counterterrorism initiatives since 9/11 have focused on preventing further attacks." He nodded. "There were these guys and others. What's your point?"

"Since the whole intelligence community, including you guys, came under the Director of National Intelligence, I assume you're aware that the hunt for and prosecution of home-grown terrorists has stepped up quite intensely. We need to move faster."

"Are we supposed to move faster at the expense of accuracy in our investigations?"

"The American people are terrified. Hell, we had a bombing at the goddam Olympics in Atlanta. Who knows where they'll strike next? And by they, I mean these crazy liberals who are siding with our enemies."

"Sir, every one of our investigations is moving ahead with all due haste."

The US Attorney leaned forward, hands clasped on his desk. "Really? And what happens if your idea of 'all due haste' isn't fast enough and this guy, Yusuf Abdullah, and his accomplices funnel enough money to the Middle East to, say, blow up soldiers on a U.S. base there? You want the blood and that failure on your hands?"

The agent cleared his throat. "No, but I don't want to ruin the lives of innocent people either. You know that once someone is even accused, the public is hyped up enough now to believe they're guilty, whether they are or not. We're trying to not make mistakes.

"And," he continued, "what about this? What if your men jumping in ahead of us and questioning everyone scares them into destroying records and going underground?"

The US Attorney smiled.

"You." The agent stopped short of calling him a bastard. "You sent your guys in to force our hand and get us to move faster, didn't you?"

"Bring me convictable bodies. They're pressuring all of us to increase our numbers. The public demands it."

"That's bullshit. The politicians are the ones demanding it. More convictions, no matter what. Because they know that's what will get them re-elected."

"I have an important phone appointment in," the U.S. Attorney looked at his watch, "two minutes. Just go do your damn job."

Stepping outside in the fresh air, the agent thought about being an innocent man sent to prison, having his life ruined, and a new thought crossed his mind.

If this is what they're demanding now, do I still want to do this job?

Quickly, he dismissed it.

Another thought arose, about the U.S. Attorney, and stuck with him.

It'll be a big coup for you personally, won't it? if you rack up a huge number of scalps and then run for office on a law-and-order platform.

*

Jen was waiting, leaning on the edge of her desk and looking anxious, when Dave arrived on Monday at eight forty-five.

"We need to talk."

"Can I get into my office first?" He was aware of sounding irritated, and backed up. "Sorry. We just had our weekend ruined."

"That makes two of us."

When he dropped his briefcase on his desk, he motioned her to have a seat, but she remained on her feet and paced.

"I came in here Saturday afternoon for some work files I'd forgotten, and when I walked back outside, a black car was parked across the street. Dave, they were taking pictures of the building of me."

"My legs went weak, and a guy stepped out of the passenger side and crossed the street toward me. I froze, and asked him, 'Who are you? Why are you taking my picture?' He said, 'Investigator.' I should have asked for an I.D. I mean, an investigator for whom? But I was shaken up."

"What did he want?"

"He started firing questions, pretty forcefully, like he was trying to intimidate me into answering without thinking. He asked how many exits there were from this building. Is there a back alley? Did I know if there were any weapons inside?"

"Oh my god, Jen."

"I said there's a back door from the kitchen outside and no, of course, there aren't any weapons in here. Are there?"

He stared at her. "Of course not. Why would you even ask me that? Hell, I don't even own a gun."

She put her hands on her cheeks, which were flushed now. "I'm sorry. I don't know. He kept firing questions. How long I've worked for you? What my duties are? But I got ahold of myself and stopped answering and he stopped. Dave, I'm so upset about the fact that they're watching all of us. I'm just a little paranoid."

"What do you mean watching all of us?"

"Mary is in the kitchen. She's a mess. Go talk to her."

Jen followed him, and they found Mary sitting at the kitchen table, eyes red, staring at the floor.

Dave squatted beside her. "Something happened. What?"

She wouldn't make eye contact.

"Tell me."

"I overheard Jen telling you just now," she finally replied. "It was probably the same guy who stopped me on my way out on Friday, after Jen was gone."

"And what happened?"

"I—I answered him when he asked about Yusuf Abdullah."

"What did he ask?"

"If I had any kind of personal knowledge about the work being done here on his behalf and I didn't want to lie, I don't know, my mind scrambled. He was so forceful, I felt overwhelmed. I said, 'Yes.' I mean, I didn't want to say 'no' and be caught in a lie later somehow."

"And?"

"He said, 'Do not leave town. You'll need to make a statement and it will look very bad if you try to avoid questioning.'"

When Dave stood, Jen was drumming her fingers on the kitchen counter.

"From now on, it's 'no comment.' That's it," Jen said, looking calm again and determined. "That's what I should have said. You, too, Mary. You know that's a legitimate option, right?"

Mary took several long, slow breaths. "I do now. It's just that they were so intimidating."

Dave was aware that his own breathing had become shallow. *Whoever* they *are.*

*

"No, I'm not ignoring you," Dave insisted that Saturday, on the drive to Daisy's and Jack's place. "But how do I know what I'm 'lawyering up' for, if no one's even told me why they're really focusing on Abdullah? It can't be because we left a few details off an application form."

Normally, they would be wrangling over the radio, switching between sports talk and easy listening. Neither had turned it on.

Hannah looked exasperated. "Just get the name of a defense lawyer. That's all I'm saying. We're under surveillance; your staff is being questioned by some government agency, and you can be sure it isn't the postal service. Come on. Why are you hesitating?"

He tapped the steering wheel. *Because I don't know who or what I'm up against. And I'm not being accused of anything.*

What was going on right now felt like shadow boxing, which made him unsure and off his game. So, what was he going to say to a lawyer, "Someone's keeping an eye on me, but I don't know who?" Better to be fully armed with as much information as possible.

"While you're *taking your sweet time thinking* about it," Hannah said, "we should try to look and sound as if nothing bad is going on while we're visiting with Daisy and Jack today. She's excited to show us all the pictures from the wedding and some they took on the islands on their honeymoon. Plus, they've done some work on the house."

Right there, he thought, *is the reason he wasn't reacting yet.* Just as she felt the need to keep things on an even keel for their family, he felt the same need to remain calm for all their sakes.

Which worked until Daisy walked them out to the car at the end of the afternoon.

"Gorgeous pictures," said Hannah, kissing Daisy on the cheek.

Dave stepped in for a hug. "Great cookout, sweetheart. The

steaks were perfect, and you and Jack have really made the house look great."

She hugged him and stepped back. "And you two look absolutely like you're hiding something. Dad, you bounced your leg all day, which always means you're anxious. And mom, your smile was thin as paper and your laugh was fake. What the hell is going on? One of you isn't seriously ill, are you?"

Hannah pressed her lips together, then let the words out in a flood.

"Your father is being watched by the government. They even followed us on our weekend getaway. It was terrible. They're watching his office too. They think he's involved with someone... who," she added, "has probably done something really wrong."

So much for "trying to look and sound as if nothing bad is going on." Dave was not prepared to handle Daisy being inundated with this news. It would add more pressure.

"It's going to be fine. Nothing bad is going to happen."

"Dad, are you kidding? This sounds really serious," Daisy shot back. "You can't just sit there and do nothing. Who's watching you, and why? What does your lawyer say? What's he doing about this?"

"Your father doesn't want to contact a lawyer yet."

Daisy ran her hands through her hair. "Dad, you can't be your usual Mr. Cool, Calm, and Logical self about this. You've got to get ahead of it."

Too late, he thought, realizing his hands had just gone slightly cold. The emotion that had tried to well up and take over for days, like it was trying now, was the biggest reason why he was keeping a lid on things. Emotion could swamp logic, and this was a time when he would need logic to fight for himself.

"Tell him," Hannah seconded.

"You've got to get in touch with a good criminal defense lawyer."

Dave balked. "But I'm not a criminal."

"I know that, and you know that. But if the government thinks you are or might be, you sure as hell better be ready to defend yourself."

"Jack has a friend who was wrongly accused of embezzling from his firm," she pressed, "and a really good defense lawyer proved him innocent when the board of directors wanted his head on a platter. Turned out someone had created false evidence against him, and they went to jail. He'll get the contact info and text you."

Great, Dave thought, driving home. *Now my new son-in-law will wonder what his daughter's old man has been up to. That's just perfect.*

Hannah reached across and squeezed his arm. "You're mad at me, aren't you? Tell me what you're thinking."

"I'm thinking I need a double martini."

"And…?"

"And when Jack sends the contact info, I'll make an appointment."

"*Good.*"

"How about you? What are you thinking?"

She looked like she wanted to be anywhere but in this mess.

"I'll join you for that double martini. And first thing Monday morning, you reach out to a lawyer and get ahead of this."

"If I can."

"Let's stay positive. Of course, you can."

*

The doorbell rang again, and Mary nearly burned her hand taking the casserole dish out of the oven. Her father's favorite. Baked ziti. It would have time to cool a little since her parents were just now at the door, a little early for dinner.

Two men in gray suits greeted her, displaying badges identifying them, one as an FBI agent, the other as an IRS agent. Both were wearing pistols in shoulder holsters.

"I'm from IRS Criminal Investigation Division, Agent Murphy. Mary Carter, we need to talk with you.

Mary looked up and down the street. Were neighbors watching? Where were her parents and what would they think when they showed up?

Seated on the living room sofa, Agent Murphy launched the questioning. "You are the one who prepared the application for the charitable organization named Bread for Children Foundation, is that correct?"

She noticed the FBI agent had taken out a small pad and pen and was ready to make notes.

"I was, yes," she said, trying to sound calm.

"I want you to explain your level of involvement in the process."

Her explanation sounded lame and stumbling to her, like it was coming from someone who was making up the answer as she went along.

"I'm sorry," she said, when she was finished, "but as you can see, I'm a bit nervous. I've never had criminal investigators in my home or asking me questions before. Ever."

"And this is a criminal investigation, just to be perfectly clear. We're looking into the organization I named and all of its officers and persons involved with the formation and operation of the entity. That includes David Mattson," he paused, "and you."

"I didn't have anything to do with the formation or operation of Dr. Abdullah's foundation. I work in Mr. Mattson's accounting firm, and I was just following instructions, filling out the form as best I could, and..." she realized what she was about to say, and stopped. She felt her hands trembling.

"What can you tell us about Dr. Abdullah's meeting with Mr. Mattson at his office?" Apparently noticing she was anxious, he gave her a minute to calm herself.

"Please describe the entire process, starting with when Yusuf Abdullah met with David Mattson."

Wracking her brain for details, she described the meeting between Dave and Yusuf, and also her meeting with Dave after Yusuf left, wanting to show herself as honest and cooperative as possible.

"So, Mr. Mattson told you he didn't have time to fill out the application, and passed it off to you? Wouldn't that mean you are responsible for everything on the application?"

This felt like a trick question, a trap.

"It means that while I was responsible for filling out the questionnaire, I was not responsible for originating that information."

"Where did the information come from?"

Through the front picture window, she saw her parents get out of their Chevy and start up the front walk.

"I referred questions I didn't know how to answer to Mr. Mattson."

"I want you to answer this question carefully, because I'm going to ask you again. For the record. Did you personally supply any of the information that went onto the application?"

"No. Not directly. I mean, I didn't fabricate anything, if that's what you're also asking."

The front door swung open a little, and her father's face appeared, smiling. "Mare, hi! We're here. We didn't know you were having other company this evening."

She motioned for them to come in. "Why don't you and mom go into the kitchen?" she said hurriedly. "I'll be done in a moment, I think."

Agent Murphy waited until her parents had passed through, ignoring their curious glances.

"Just a few more questions, for now."

Mary was fighting tears. What would she tell her parents?

"Is it your statement now that you did not originate or create any of the information used to complete the application in question?"

Why was he asking this again?

"No, I did not," she replied, steadying her voice.

"Who supplied you with the information you used?"

Here it was—the real point of their visit. She could sense it.

"It was supplied by Mr. Mattson."

"So, he told you how to respond."

This felt like very tricky ground.

"He answered the questions I asked him," she responded, trying not to sound defensive. "He didn't *direct me*—as in, he didn't review the form and tell me to change answers he didn't like."

"Mary," Agent Murphy said, pulling a form out of a leather folder, "is this the form you prepared for the Bread for Children Foundation?"

She took it from his hand and scanned it carefully. "Yes."

"Are there any errors that you're aware of in this

application?"

"Well, since I just worked from the information that was given to me, I can't say for sure. There could be. But I don't know that."

Murphy frowned. "Can you explain that statement?"

"The application was started by someone at another accounting firm before the file was given to Mr. Mattson to complete. So, much of the information came from them."

"Do you know why the other firm did not complete the application?"

For the first time, the FBI agent spoke. "That would be hearsay."

Murphy pulled another document from the leather folder, and handed her a copy of a letter from the previous accountant. "Have you ever seen this before?"

"I have. The original was in the file we received."

"Is there anything else you need to tell us? This would be a good time."

"No, I have nothing more to say."

Murphy rose.

"Mary, you are not to disclose this meeting to anyone. You've been helpful, and if you continue to assist with this investigation, I'll put in a good word to the U.S. Attorney to treat you as a witness and not a possible defendant."

"I haven't done anything wrong. Neither has Mr. Mattson. He passed along whatever information he had and helped me get an application out just ahead of an important deadline. That's all."

The FBI agent had risen from his seat as well, and was no longer taking notes.

"As I said," Agent Murphy concluded, "I'll do my best to

keep you out of the forthcoming criminal charges if you continue to cooperate. Which means telling no one about this visit. And I mean no one."

"Where is Mary this morning?" Dave asked Jen, when he found her in the office's kitchen.

"I don't know. Why?" Jen replied, stirring honey into a mug of tea.

"Because she's always here early, and I don't see her in her workspace."

"True. She is an early bird."

Dave was thinking about his plans for an early retirement. Could it start today?

In an hour, Jen stepped into Dave's office. "You know it's ten, and Mary's still not here. I called her home and her cell, and she's not answering. She would have told me if she knew she was going to be late this morning. I hope she's not sick or has been in an accident."

Dave's mind was elsewhere. He stared at the small slip of paper lying on his desk, with the name and number of the criminal defense attorney Jack's friend recommended highly. Probably expensive as hell. A full day had passed between Hannah's and Daisy's assault on him to get a lawyer and he had more than halfway talked himself out of it. He folded the paper and tucked it in his shirt pocket.

"Let me know when you find out if she's okay and coming in. I have another project for her."

He relaxed in his chair, enjoying the fact that, after a series of stressful days, his first meeting was not for another hour. Rellerson's was a regional sporting goods chain and a big client. He wanted to be focused and calm when their business manager arrived.

He had not seen the unmarked car following him to the office earlier, nor had he witnessed it pulling over to the curb to wait for the right moment.

*

The sound of the front door banging open coincided with Dave sighting two men in helmets and tactical gear running past his window, followed a few seconds later by the sound of the building's back door into the kitchen slamming open.

He was already on his feet when Jen burst into his office, just ahead of two men in gray suits. Through the open doorway, he could see out into the reception area, where two more men in tactical gear were scanning the room, with automatic weapons at the ready. He could hear the two who had stormed in through the back door calling out, "*All clear.*"

"Who are you?" he demanded of the gray suits. "*What the hell is going on?*"

"Sit," said one of them, as they both produced badges.

Dave fought to calm himself down and gestured to the two armchairs in his office. "Please take a seat. You startled me." A show of non-resistance was clearly in order.

He noticed that beneath their coats, they had shoulder holsters, which were unsnapped in case they needed quick access to their firearms.

"Can you snap those back up? There are no weapons here."

They did not respond.

Jen was backing out of the room, and one of them said to her, "Go back to your desk. Do not leave these premises."

One of the men in tactical gear stuck his head in Dave's office and spoke to the gray suit, who seemed to be in charge.

"Agent Murphy, the building is clear. No sign of any weapons or forces that would offer resistance."

The two men snapped their shoulder holsters.

"Thanks. Two of you stay out there with the receptionist. Two of you go out to the sidewalk and stay there with the others."

Others?

From where he was seated behind his desk, Dave craned his neck to see out the window to the front of the building.

Ten or twelve men in suits, all wearing shoulder holsters with weapons, were lined up along the sidewalk out front.

"Yes, those are federal agents, Mr. Mattson. There are more on the street that back this property should anyone attempt a back-door escape."

"Escape for what reason? I haven't done anything wrong. I don't even know what you want. Isn't this swat team thing a bit of overkill?"

From the look on Agent Murphy's face, Dave could see he pressed the wrong button.

"We ask the questions. You give the answers."

He thought about calling Hannah… or the police… or someone… and glanced at the phone.

"No phone calls. Just answers."

Dave's mind was reeling and he felt trapped. His temples were pounding.

All the questions fired at him related to Yusuf Abdullah—no surprise. He had felt this coming, hadn't he? Maybe not this SWAT team corralling him at his office, but these questions.

Every question brought denials.

No, he answered, he had not been part of an organized plan to defraud the U.S. Government by helping a foreign agent—was Abdullah acting on behalf of a foreign and malign force?—to wrongfully secure American services in the support of terrorists.

No, he did not know Abdullah was transferring tens of thousands of dollars from America to 'foreign entities.'

No, ridiculous as it now sounded even to him, he really did not know if Abdullah's so-called non-profit group was a charitable organization or something else, say, a paramilitary group.

Somewhere in the midst of all the questions, Dave thought of Mary. It was clear they had questioned her first, which explained her absence today, because some of the questions could only have come from someone in this office with knowledge about how the postal application was prepared.

As that thought occurred, he heard the sound of a helicopter overhead. Armed reinforcements? Did they come prepared for a shoot-out?

Agent Murphy was now more hostile-sounding.

"And so, your statement to us is, though you knew nothing about Dr. Abdullah's activities whatsoever, you participated in creating a bogus application for non-profit status so that he could continue to raise funds for overseas operations—*is that correct?*"

The question was colored by Agent Murphy's wording, "overseas operations." Clearly, he was trying to get Dave to confess involvement with foreign subversives, which would amount to treason.

His throat went dry. And in the back of Dave's mind, he could hear Hannah and Daisy shouting at him, telling him what to say next.

"I want to speak with my lawyer." Dave reached for his phone, fumbling in his pocket for the phone number he had copied from Jack's message early this morning.

"I'm sorry, Mr. Mattson, but we are not finished here."

"I believe I have the right."

"Under the Patriot Act, we do not have to allow you access to your lawyer while you're under questioning."

"You've asked me every question three or four times. I have nothing more to tell you. Now I *want* to speak with my lawyer."

Agent Murphy stood and dropped a subpoena on Dave's desk. "This is going to give us all the information we need about your activities."

Scanning the document quickly, Dave saw that it gave them the power to take any and all records, papers or documents for Yusuf and his wife, for all of their personal accounting and business activities, as well as the charity application file for Bread for Children. They were also allowed to copy any and all computer records for the same.

When Dave looked up, Agent Murphy was staring him in the eye. Clearly, he was determined to find something.

"Mr. Mattson, you're only being brought into this case as a witness."

Dave nodded. *What a load of bullshit! Why do I feel like you just put a noose around my neck?*

If these men needed to bring back evidence against Yusuf Abdullah and anyone connected with him, he suspected they would do everything in their power to find whatever tiny shred of "evidence" they could dig up.

When the men were finished rifling the files, Agent Murphy faced him again. "These are all the files pertaining to Dr. Abdullah, correct? There are no others?"

"You scoured every cabinet and drawer. I'm sure you have everything."

How is this intensive intrusion not some kind of violation of his rights? He wanted to say, *"Did you even leave any paint on the file cabinets?"*

*

At 12.02, when Dave arrived home, shaken, Hannah's car was there. He found her in the family room, where she had the TV turned on to an Albany station. Almost before they could speak, they saw Daisy pull into the driveway.

"*Breaking news.* We still have no word," said the natty young reporter, "as to why a swat team of federal agents surrounded an office in Saratoga Springs this morning, but our news helicopter got this footage."

There was Dave's office, viewed from above, and the tactical unit surrounding the building.

The co-anchor picked up the story. "We do know the office building they surrounded houses an accounting firm owned by David Mattson, a Saratoga resident. What was going on in that building, we have no idea. There are no reports of arrests, not yet anyway."

Hannah grabbed Dave, squeezing him tightly. "Ohmygod, ohmygod, ohmygod…"

Daisy was at their side now, hugging both of them. "Dad, what happened? Are you okay? Is Jen okay?"

"I called Jen's husband to come get her. She was too shaken up to drive home."

"What about Mary?"

"She didn't come in. They already got to her."

The news anchor went on. "We can't speculate as to why federal agents descended on this business, but sources tell us an investigation is underway about possible ties between this accounting firm, yes, a small hometown firm and foreign nationals…"

"*Bastards*," Daisy shouted. "You can't 'speculate,' but you can report what 'sources' told you? They're pressuring you by leaking tidbits to the media, and these imbeciles are only too happy to exploit a factoid even a false one and turn it into a hot story." She let fly a string of curse words.

Dave's mind felt numb, the room felt hazy, and it was hard to breathe.

Daisy pressed a phone into his hand.

He stared at her.

"*Call… the… lawyer.*"

Chapter 7

"From the way you're describing this swat, you were not being brought into this case as a witness. You're a suspect."

The lawyer, S. Carl King, pressed his hands together on top of his desk. "They're allowed to tell you that."

"What does that mean? They told me if I lied to them as federal agents, that's a felony."

"Absolutely true. But they're allowed to lie to you to obtain the information they're after. Lovely one-way street, isn't it?"

Dave swore.

"Now tell me," Carl pressed, "exactly what happened—every single thing you can recall, every question they asked you."

Dave gripped the arms of the chair, angry. "I feel like my rights were violated all over the place. They tipped off the media, and now I'm probably already guilty in the eyes of the public. My wife and daughter are afraid to go out anywhere for fear of being harassed."

King studied him before answering. "Since the Patriot Act was passed, it's clear that the rights of an American citizen can be suspended when the government deems it 'necessary' in the interest of national security. You can stop insisting on your rights from here on out, all three of you, and we can focus here. I can only help if you tell me everything."

After a long and detailed account of his connection with Yusuf Abdullah, Dave stopped for a breather. "Look, I've known Yusuf for twenty years. I trust the guy. On the other hand, right now, I wish I'd never set eyes on him."

"That's the whole idea behind the swat and show of force. To unsettle or break that connection and get you to turn on Dr. Abdullah. You're more likely to panic and give them something to help hang the guy. They've got to go back to the U.S. Attorney with a case to try. He needs scalps."

"But the chances of finding some irregularity in almost anyone's files are pretty high. Even people who try really hard to go by all the rules get conflicting information from the government and its agencies. Sometimes their contradictions create the so-called problem."

Carl said, "That's true, but it's not the point right now. Stay focused. Keep going."

An hour later, when all the agents' questions and his answers were out, Dave came back to his relationship with Dr. Abdullah.

"I'm telling you, this guy has always been clean."

"You'd vouch for him? In court?"

"Yusuf was audited by the I.R.S. just two years ago. The I.R.S. made it very contentious, then I never suspected what was really up. I walked through the whole thing with him, and it ended well. They were trying hard to find something, but they didn't. Case closed."

"Or so you thought. This is bigger. A lot bigger. They're looking at him and, most likely, at you as agents of a foreign entity. Not a friendly one."

Dave felt a cold sweat start. "What do we do? Where do we start?"

Carl pushed a paper across his desk. "We start with you signing this document, hiring me as your legal representative."

Dave pulled the paper in front of him and stared at it. "Then what?—I mean, what do *I* do?"

"You go back to your office and carry on just as you usually would. No trips out of town. Stay off the phone; it's tapped for sure. I'll get to work on your behalf. You act normal."

With someone trying to hang me, act normal?

"Will do," Dave said, trying not to sound as bitter and caustic as he felt.

*

There was no chance of returning to a normal work setting.

Three news vans were parked across the street from Dave's office, and he drove past them, went three blocks and turned right. Coming down the street behind his building, he parked and walked through an alley beside the building behind him, past dumpsters, and into his building's back lot, rushing across the lawn and dashing in the back door.

Behaving like a guy with something to hide.

Damn this situation.

Jen was in the kitchen when he entered. "Not surprised to see you coming in this way. I walked right past the reporters and didn't respond to any of their questions, not even the loud, pushy woman who kept shoving a microphone in my face."

"Jen, I am so sorry—"

"It's not your fault, Dave," she interrupted. "I know you didn't do anything wrong. I know you were swamped and overwhelmed when Yusuf pressured you into helping him, and that Mary did the best she could do."

Her face had flushed and she sounded angry.

"All this pressure they're putting on you, it's just wrong. How could our own government do this to one of its citizens?"

"What matters to me," said Dave, "is that you don't get

dragged into it. I feel terrible for Mary."

"She called in 'sick' again. I won't be surprised if she quits."

Dave swore under his breath. It occurred to him that he'd never sworn so much in his life and if his mother were alive, she'd be appalled. Or maybe she would swear, too. In the back of his mind, he hoped word of this mess wouldn't reach his dad down in Florida.

"Don't worry about me," Jen finished. "If they show up again, I'm walking out and going home. They can arrest me if they want to."

"Let's hope they don't. Show up, I mean."

*

Three minutes later, when Dave had settled at his desk, he heard the front door open and, even though his closed office door, he caught the edge in Jen's voice.

He stood, to step out and see what was going on, but his door opened and Agent Murphy strode in, making sure his shoulder holster and sidearm were visible. Before he could say a word, Murphy ordered him.

"Sit."

Refusing to be intimidated, Dave complied but sat upright in his chair, leaning forward a little.

I will not let him think I'm intimidated or cowed.

In the back of his mind, though, he could hear Hannah's and Daisy's voices along with Carl King's, all saying, *"Don't act belligerent. Don't give them a reason to increase the pressure on you."* Easy for them, when he wanted to punch Agent Murphy.

"How can I help you today?"

"If you're trying to hide from us, there's no need. All the

streets around here are being monitored for your movements. I hope the backyard here isn't muddy. You could ruin your dress shoes trying to dodge us."

Dave kept his expression neutral.

"How can I help you?"

Agent Murphy pulled a chair up across from Dave's desk.

"You can answer this. Did you know Yusuf Abdullah was sending money overseas? To Iraq?"

Dave had checked out the window and did not see the SWAT team of federal agents today. That was a relief, at least.

"I believe I already answered that question."

"Mr. Mattson, you'll answer my questions until I'm satisfied, I have complete and honest answers from you. Which I'm not. Did you know?"

A surge of impatience rose, and Dave picked up the phone receiver to call Carl King.

Agent Murphy lunged forward and jammed his finger down on the button hanging up the phone.

"What are you doing?" Dave shot back. "I can call my lawyer if..."

"Apparently you didn't get the message the last time I was here. You can do what I *say* you can do. Put down the receiver, or we'll have this conversation in a secure facility in Albany or Washington. Your choice, and I suggest you choose wisely. You see, the thing is, I can take you away for questioning somewhere and I don't have to let you call Hannah or Daisy to let them know where you are."

Hearing their names so obviously used to intimidate him further, David had to push down his rising fury. "So, you're going to threaten me. Why are you treating me like this?"

Agent Murphy's expression turned hostile.

"Answer my questions," his voice was a low growl, "or take a long ride and answer them somewhere else."

For the next hour, a barrage of the same questions he'd answered before came at him.

"Are you aware that Bread for Children Foundation was sending money to Iraq?"

"I have no knowledge of that."

Agent Murphy kept looking at his legal pad.

"Last time, you just said, 'No.'"

"'No'... 'I have no knowledge of it'... same answer," Dave responded, standing his ground.

He's trying to make me think I'm contradicting myself. This was getting tricky.

"No knowledge or no *direct* knowledge? Perhaps Mary knew and mentioned it. Remember, before you answer, we've taken her official statement. If you knew and didn't report it, you're culpable for covering up fraud and possibly treason."

For a split second, this threw him. Was it possible she'd said something to him about what Yusuf was doing? Had she called Yusuf's office for information to fill out the application, and learned something about a transfer of funds... then mentioned it to him?

He felt warm under the collar. Again, Agent Murphy was trying to throw him off-balance and it was clearly watching his every small movement. He forced himself not to move a muscle.

"Are you aware," Murphy pressed on, "of the fact that Bread for Children Foundation was telling potential contributors the entity was a registered charitable organization and that all contributions were tax deductible?"

"I was not, and have never been, aware of that or of any other activities of the foundation that you're asking me about," Dave responded, and added, "not directly *or* indirectly."

He wanted to say, *Write that in your notes*, but bit his tongue.

When Agent Murphy was gone, ending with the reminder, "Do not travel anywhere out of town," Dave sat on the edge of Jen's desk.

"Can you believe?"

She held an index finger up to his lips.

He stared at her as she slid a paper across her desk, with the handwritten message,

We have to be careful with what we say. We can't be sure they haven't planted a listening device.

He fumbled with what to say next, but she helped him out.

"Would you mind if I took an early lunch?" she raised her eyebrows. "I ordered in."

By calling for pizza delivery, it appeared they convinced the waiting reporters out front that they were eating in. After a big show of paying and tipping the driver at the front door, they slipped out the back, heading toward the next street over where Dave's car was parked.

"Oh, we're not taking your car," said Jen. "See the Ford F-150 that just pulled in?" She nodded toward the driveway they were approaching across the back lawn of the accounting office. "That's my son, Jamie. I called him to pick us up. The federal agents are watching your vehicle. We'll be followed."

"Jen, I don't want to get you more involved in this."

"More involved than me being followed to and from work? Knowing that my home phone could be tapped?"

Dave winced.

*

Standing at the hostess station in the local barbecue restaurant, waiting to be seated, Jen breathed a sigh of relief. "We made it through the gauntlet."

Through the lunch crowd, Dave noticed a long-time business acquaintance, Jerry Hammet, whose wife had worked with Hannah on a hospital fundraiser. They'd become friends during a stint when they'd played cards with some other guys a couple nights a month, and Jerry and Lisa had come to Daisy and Jack's wedding. It was good to see a friendly face.

"Follow me," said the hostess, menus in hand, leading them to a table.

As they passed the table where Jerry was seated with two other men, Dave stopped and let Jen go on with the hostess.

"Sorry we didn't have much time to chat at the wedding," Dave said, extending his hand. "Hope you had a good time. How's it going?"

Jerry glanced across the table at the two men with him, glanced around the restaurant as if checking to see who was watching, then looked up at Dave. He didn't shake Dave's hand.

"Everything's fine."

There was awkwardness.

"Lisa and the boys, okay? Hannah said, your oldest just got into med school."

Jerry nodded, avoiding eye contact. "Hey, Dave, these guys and I are in the middle of something."

The distinct cold-shoulder vibe struck, and Dave forced a smile.

"Got it. Enjoy your lunch, gentlemen."

Shouldering his way past servers with full trays, passing crowded tables and booths, he glanced side-to-side, to see if he knew anyone else here. Anyone else who Jerry's response made it plain now wanted to avoid being seen with him. He felt his stomach dropping and his face and hands going cold.

Sliding into the booth opposite Jen, he ignored the menu lying on the table.

Jen frowned. "What's wrong? You look pale. Are you all right?"

"No. I don't feel so good." He swallowed hard, to keep down the bile churning up from his stomach.

"Was it something Jerry said to you?"

"It's what he didn't say. But I got the message loud and clear."

Jen set down her menu. "To be honest, I'm not feeling comfortable here. Let's give up the booth and order takeout."

"You order. I don't think I can eat."

*

"Maybe you were interrupting an important business lunch," Hannah insisted that evening.

"He wouldn't shake my hand. Wouldn't look at me. After knowing this guy for years, now I'm a rabid dog."

Hannah was silent, and turned to stare out the dining room window.

Neither of them had touched their favorite crab soup, which she'd brought home for dinner. When she turned back to face him, her eyes were filling with tears, and she looked angry.

"I haven't told you…"

He leaned toward her and laid his hand on hers. "What? Don't tell me Agent Murphy showed up and harassed you at work?"

She wiped her nose with the napkin. "No. Though I suppose

I should expect that could happen, shouldn't I?"

It hit him just exactly how uncertain and precarious their lives had suddenly become. No place felt safe.

"Well," Hannah ventured, "two days ago, some of the women at work were planning a baby shower for Kara. She's due in a month. They were standing around the coffee machine, planning who would be in charge of what, and I walked up and offered to help."

Dave could feel what was coming.

"Everyone went silent. I thought maybe they hadn't heard me because they'd all been jabbering away, and I offered again.—Nothing. That's when it hit me."

Dave sat back and dropped his head in his hands.

"Bev motioned me away from the group, and when we were alone, she said, 'You have to realize that most of these women are uncomfortable around you now. I'm not,' she said. 'But it would be best if you backed off.'"

Dave looked up. "That was nice of Bev."

"*Nice?*" Hannah shot back, her eyes flashing. "She was lying. She's avoiding me, too. She just wanted to sound like she's such a good person that she'll even stand by a… a…"

"The wife of a traitor?"

Hannah sat back, looking horrified. "Don't say that. Don't use that word. You're not a traitor."

"We seem to be the only people—besides Daisy, Jack, and Jen—who know that."

*

"Are you okay being seen with me," Dave said, looking around the sun room of the nursing home, where he found Evelyn the next afternoon.

Evelyn snorted and waved her hand at the few other residents seated randomly around. "Half of them can't see or hear, and the other half don't know what day it is."

"Be nice."

"That is being nice. Are you asking if it's okay because you've made your big TV debut and you think your adoring fans will rush in on us?"

"You saw the news."

She motioned for him to sit in the upholstered chair beside hers.

"I'm just happy you didn't do something ridiculous and stay away because you think you're protecting me, which you aren't. One of the men in gray was here three days ago."

"Damn. Evelyn, I'm so sorry. What happened?"

She tapped the empty water glass on the small table between them. "This needs something in it. Then I talk, and not until. You know where the bottle is in my room."

When they were sipping Glenfiddich, she sat back with a self-satisfied smile.

"What is it people say these days? I tore him a new one."

Dave nearly spewed his sip of scotch.

"Oh, dear lord, what did you say?"

"Agent Murphy, so arrogant. So sure of his power. He kept asking the same questions, over and over. I asked him if he was getting senile and did he forget he'd already asked me these questions?

"That made him angry, and he had the nerve to bring up my father and how he knew my father had been investigated under suspicion of 'unamerican activities.'"

Dave saw her face color. "Bastard."

"I said, 'How dare you mention my father and that terrible, terrible business? If you bring that up again, I'll do damage to you with my cane.'"

"*Evelyn.*"

"Then that little... *Mussolini*... said another threat like that could land me in prison." She squared her shoulders and sounded authoritarian. "'*I* am a federal agent.'"

"He *is* a federal agent. You need to be careful."

"Careful? I said, 'I don't care if you're the Holy Trinity. I'll knock that power-mad smirk off your face. You can threaten me with prison all you want. I'm already in prison. It's called a ninety-six-year-old body. Now get out. It's time for bingo.'"

Dave sipped his scotch. "Please tell me you didn't say all that."

"She did," came a small voice from a sofa twenty feet away. The old man's eyes were full of mirth. "I overheard every word of it. What a performance. Kate Hepburn couldn't have done better."

Evelyn tossed back the last of her scotch.

"Oh, Albert, you're only saying that because it's true."

An hour later, as he left, Dave took Evelyn's hand gently, feeling disheartened.

"You may be our only friend left."

"Nonsense. People will back away right at the start because they don't know what to say or they're a bit nervous and ducking for cover. But your true friends are still there. Give them time to show their heads."

At home, Hannah dragged it out of him. "They got to Evelyn, too, didn't they?"

"They questioned her. But you couldn't exactly say they *got* to her."

She raised her eyebrows in question.

"Let's just say the American forces needed her on D-Day."

*

Jerry Hammett tried to sound calm and collected, but his throat was dry and his words sounded croaky.

"I told you last week. I really don't know Dave Mattson well enough to comment on his character."

The federal agent kept staring at him, and Jerry shifted uneasily in his chair.

"Do your co-workers know anything about your friendship with Mattson? I can ask them what they know about you two."

"I've told you a number of times, I don't know him that well."

"But you and your wife were invited to his daughter's wedding."

Hammett felt sick. "What is it you want me to tell you?"

The agent shrugged. "Have you ever had a reason to suspect Mattson isn't honest? Ever suspected he takes money under the table?"

Hammett hesitated. "Is that what you want me to say?"

"That would be priming the witness and that's illegal," said the agent.

"But if I say something like that, you'll stop showing up here? I mean, I can't have my employees thinking I'm involved with this... This huge mess Mattson's got himself into."

The agent tapped his pencil on his notepad. "There must be something you can tell me."

*

Hannah looked like she might be sick, but she looked at Dave with concern. "You're home early."

"It was a rough day."

"This story they're reporting won't make it any easier." She nodded at the TV with its early, network news broadcast from the affiliate in Albany.

"We have this important story, coming in from our affiliate in Grand Rapids, where federal agents say they've uncovered a terrorist sleeper cell. Seems they're being discovered all over the U.S. Here's more, from Claire Rembeaux in Grand Rapids."

Dave's temples were pounding. "I don't know if we need to see this right now." He reached for the remote.

Hannah's hand shot out and she pulled it away. "It's frightening, Dave, but I think we absolutely need to see this."

"After a preliminary hearing in federal court here today, a lawyer claims that his client, a young Muslim, new to this country, is being *set up* for prosecution by the U.S. Government. His client, Elias Koutab, from Egypt, who arrived in Grand Rapids five years ago, is pleading with the public to know he is innocent."

The story was cut to pre-taped footage of Koutab, a man in his early thirties, with the reporter's voice-over.

"Elias Koutab works as a file clerk in county offices by day and as a re-stock man in a local grocery store by night, doing his best to support a young family that includes his wife and two small boys. On weekends, he does what many young men do he's a devoted father to his sons."

The footage showed him taking turns pushing three little boys on swings, and throwing a frisbee with them. Then it cut to Koutab.

"Between work and studying for a degree in biology and giving time to family, I hardly have time to sleep," he said, his young wife at his side looking terrified. "When, where and how am I committing acts of terror? Which I would never do. I came to the United States because I love this great country and only want to make a good life here for my family."

"But," the reporter cut in, "according to documents filed by the government in federal court here, "Koutab has been aiding and abetting foreign entities in this country who are on the terrorist watch list because of violent activities against American facilities overseas."

A new face appeared on screen, with the tagline under it, "Eric Bidington, Defense Lawyer."

"A gross injustice has already been done to my client, Mr. Koutab, because the prosecutor has claimed that the documents filed with the judge are protected under recent anti-terrorist laws due to national security reasons, and therefore we can't have access to them.

"*How*," Bidington demanded, starting into the camera, "are we to prepare to answer charges against Mr. Koutab if the government claims it has the right to conceal information thousands of pages of alleged documentation it supposedly has in its possession? We don't even know all the charges against him, so we're being kept in the dark. Unless I can shake the heavens and get access to the evidence and the charges, Mr. Koutab will go on trial without a well-prepared defense.

"I'd also like to know *how*," Bidington concluded, "this kind of backroom dealing is happening in our justice system here in America, a free and open and just society?"

The report cut to the two network anchors in Albany.

"Did our reporter in Grand Rapids say she or anyone in the

media had access to those documents or has heard what's in them?"

"No one but the judge does. And the Department of Justice has weighed in, saying this is a matter of national security and evidence cannot be revealed in court."

"This story has local relevance, too," said the first anchor, shifting focus.

"Yes, it does. Our sources say the government is conducting in-depth investigations into possible terrorist-related activities in nearby Saratoga Springs."

"Hard to believe a malign foreign power could penetrate our area. Just weeks ago, a team of federal agents surrounded..."

Hannah quickly jabbed the "off" button on the remote, and stood staring. "Can they *do* that?" she said in a hoarse whisper.

Dave was trying to take in what they had just heard and seen. "Can they charge someone and withhold evidence and information from the accused and their lawyers?" he said. "No, I'm sure that's not legal..." He stopped, his mind churning.

"But that's what the guy's lawyer just said. The prosecution and the judge are concealing evidence and other documents from him and the accused. Did you see Koutab's poor wife? She's terrified."

"That can't be right," Dave resisted.

"It's not right, but they just said that new laws have made it possible."

A dark place began to open in the back of his mind—a fearful place he couldn't let himself go to.

"Dave, I feel sick," Hannah said, reaching for his hand. "If our government has that kind of unlimited power now, if they don't even have to present what they claim is evidence against someone, then they can convict anybody they want."

Carl King pressed his lips together tightly, and seemed to be considering his reply to Dave and Hannah's barrage of questions.

"So far, they're targeting Yusuf Abdullah, not you. Keep that in mind. They're pressuring you for information, but they're after him. I know it's nerve-wracking, but hold onto the fact that you're not they're real target."

Hannah looked grim. "What about guilt by association?"

King's leather chair squeaked as he sat back. "All they have on Dave, so to speak, is one form that wasn't completed perfectly, seeking non-profit status."

"But the courts are telling defendants and their lawyers they have other evidence that they're not showing because it has to be kept top-secret," Dave insisted. "Shouldn't we be scared about that?"

"So far, the people who have been charged and convicted of terrorist activities are people the government *has* presented clear and strong evidence against."

"So far," said Hannah, but what if that's changing?"

Carl was silent for a moment, then looked at Dave. "Remember, you're enjoying lawyer-client privilege here. You can tell me the full truth. Do you have any other dealings with Yusuf Abdullah than what you've told me so far? And do you have in your possession any documents or files pertaining to him that you haven't relinquished to the agents?"

"*No*, and *no*," Dave replied vehemently.

Carl held up one hand. "Okay. I'm a good judge of people, and I was a hundred percent sure that's how you'd answer. Besides that, I was trained in the Marine Corps years ago to read facial expressions. Believe me, it's helped me in court a lot. I always know who's lying and who's telling the truth."

"And?" Dave prompted.

"I just said I know you're telling the truth." He looked between Dave and Hannah. "Of course, this is a stressful time. I absolutely get that. But you have to find a way to relax a little. You didn't do anything wrong. They have nothing against you, per se, Dave."

He leaned back in his chair again. "I can't say what will happen with Dr. Abdullah, of course. If he's involved with hostile foreign entities, he's in serious trouble. But you. With zero evidence against you, you're not going to prison."

*

Frankie's ears perked up, then the Shih Tzu leapt to his feet from beside Hannah's chair in the family room and began his sharp, high-pitched yipping, the kind that set Dave's teeth on edge.

"*Frankie*, can it?" Dave growled. "What the hell are you barking at?"

Hannah stood to look out the window, then froze.

"Ohmygod, Dave, those are federal agents coming up the front walk, aren't they?"

Before he had a chance to get up from his easy chair, there was a loud knock, almost banging on the front door.

Agent Murphy pushed past Dave into the front room.

Dave gritted his teeth and tried to keep his voice level.

"I don't mean to sound resistant, but you asked me every question under the sun, two or three times, about my connection to Dr. Abdullah when you came to my office. There can't be any questions I haven't answered."

Agent Murphy, who had been followed inside by two other men, pointed to the sofa. "Take a seat. I do have more questions."

"Did you have to come to our home now, in the evening?" Hannah insisted. "Couldn't these questions have waited until tomorrow?"

Agent Murphy ignored her and stared at Dave.

"You recently checked into purchasing airline tickets to Dubai. Why was that?"

Dave balked. "Tickets to…"

"Dubai?" Hannah finished.

Agent Murphy pressed. "You looked into a cruise leaving from Dubai and traveling through the Arabian Gulf to the United Arab Emirates and Oman. Who do you know there? Who were you going to see?"

Hannah stared at Dave, looking confused. "What's he saying?"

"A while ago, I was considering a surprise vacation for us—a cruise. We've always talked about seeing the Middle East and maybe going to Greece, too." He turned back to Agent Murphy. "But how did you know about this?"

"You should know that your friends and acquaintances are having no problem offering information. Reggie Bradford, for instance. You accidentally let it slip to him that you have a 'secret' plan to travel to the Middle East. When we visited the Bradfords, Mrs. Bradford volunteered that they both found that piece of information troubling, given the fact that you've come under investigation."

"You're harassing our friends?" Hannah raised her voice.

"I confided in Reggie that it was a secret I was keeping *from Hannah*. And it was a trip I was considering before you started this… investigation."

"After you let the plan slip, you insisted he not tell anyone. Mr. Bradford remembered that very clearly."

"That's because I didn't want his wife to know, so she wouldn't let it slip out either."

"What's interesting to me," said Agent Murphy, "is that you made this inquiry about a Middle Eastern trip after you were contacted by the U.S. Postal Service questioning your connection to Dr. Abdullah. So, I'll ask you again: what is the purpose of the travel, you're planning to the Middle East? And remember, what you say can be used as evidence."

The word *evidence* went off like a bomb in the room and Hannah was startled.

Dave barely kept his temper from boiling over. "All I was doing was planning a surprise vacation. That's the truth. Period."

Agent Murphy reached into his suitcoat pocket, and pulled out a paper. He handed it to Dave.

"This is a warrant allowing me to search your premises."

Hannah was now in tears—angry tears. "You're searching our home? For what? What do you think you'll find? Guns? Bombs?"

"If there are any," Agent Murphy said, his voice level and cool. "I assume, Mr. Mattson, that you have a home office. We'll start there."

Dave's mind raced. All they would find in his home office files were a few old manila folders with client information he probably should have tossed but hadn't in case it proved useful someday.

"If you have a warrant, I guess you can go ahead." He stood and started down the hallway. "My office is in the back of the house."

Ten minutes later, Agent Murphy looked up from a manila

folder he had rummaged out of the back of a file cabinet, with a triumphant expression. He held up a piece of paper.

"This has the name Yusuf Abdullah written across the top, and I'm going to assume this is your handwriting."

"I don't even know what that is."

"It's a list of names, phone numbers, and addresses, which I assume are people and places connected to you and Dr. Abdullah. That list is in someone else's handwriting."

Dave's mind raced back to the day months before, when he had brought home files he didn't need at the office. Why the hell hadn't he just tossed them?

"Can I see that?"

"I'll hold onto it. But maybe you can tell me. Why are the names of mosques and their addresses here? The Islamic Center of New York, Al-Sadiq Mosque. These and… eight, nine, ten other Islamic organizations."

"As best I can recall, there were… are… leaders of the Islamic community that Yusuf said he was going to contact in the interest of raising funds for his charity work."

"Why would he give this list to you?"

"Again, best I can recall, he wanted me to be familiar with these places in case representatives called to get more information from me about Dr. Abdullah and his work."

Agent Murphy's voice had remained cool the whole time he was speaking, and his eyes were expressionless. "'Best I can recall.' Vague answer. And if you're not part of his organization, why would he want people calling you?"

Murphy's emotionless delivery was now throwing Dave off. He felt like a small insect being angled into a huge web. His face got red, and he had no good answer to the agent's questions except the angry one burning in his head.

Hannah, who had slipped into the office, grabbed his arm and whispered in his ear.

"Don't say anything."

"Here's the problem, Mr. Mattson. *Your* problem, to be clear. Seems you've been planning a secretive trip to the Middle East, to nations where terrorists come from. And you lied to me when I asked you in your office if you had any other files pertaining to Dr. Abdullah anywhere else. You told me 'No' and yet I'm holding in my hand a piece of paper that says otherwise. It's plain to me you were concealing this list of potentially dangerous contacts from us."

Hannah squeezed Dave's arm tighter.

"I don't have anything to say until I speak with my lawyer," Dave managed to get out. His heart was thudding.

Agent Murphy held up the list again.

"I'll be taking this as potential evidence."

Chapter 8

Carl King kept tapping the fingers of his right hand on the desk, betraying the calm expression fixed on his face.

"He used the word 'evidence,'" Carl repeated.

"'Potential evidence,'" Dave reiterated. "And he's interviewing people from my business and our social circles. I can't begin to tell you how embarrassing this is for Hannah and me."

"Sniffing for any crumbs he can find."

"When they swatted my office, he made it sound like they had no interest in me, per se. That all this was really focused on Yusuf. Now it sounds like they're trying to drag me into whatever mess he's gotten himself into."

Carl stopped tapping his fingers and was silent for a long moment.

"There's a bigger picture we have to look at and take seriously."

"Which is?"

Carl cleared his throat. "Something big is going on in this country. Really big. I've been talking with friends in the legal world from all around the U.S. and in professional organizations I belong to. There's a round-up going on."

"What's that mean, a 'round-up'?"

"Since 9/11, the DOJ and its agents have been working double overtime to go through this country with a fine-toothed comb. They're focusing with lasers on anyone who looks middle-eastern or has middle-eastern business associates or friends."

"Profiling."

"And then some."

"I understand they want to stop terrorist attacks. I'm all for that, of course. But what if they're going too far? Seeing terrorist activity where there isn't any? I mean, if you get paranoid enough, anyone can look suspicious."

"That's the problem, and a lot of us are concerned we've now slipped into a danger zone."

"Like in the McCarthy era."

"You don't have to go back that far. Nixon was paranoid as hell and even went after movie and rock stars. John Lennon, for God's sake. Nixon thought 'Give Peace a Chance' was a call for communists to rise up. A peaceful anti-war demonstration at Kent State ended with someone leading the Ohio National Guard miscuing and ordering his men to fire, slaughtering four innocent students who were doing nothing but watching a protest. No one was ever prosecuted for that or even got a slap on the wrist."

"And you think the same paranoia is taking over now, in the aftermath of 9/11?"

"Dave, listen to this one. A guy named Raiman was suspected by the FBI of training the terrorist who flew the jetliner into the Pentagon. Though when I say 'suspected' I mean they were looking for a suspect and were determined to find one.

"Raiman was living in London, and the FBI had the British police swat Raiman's home in the middle of the night and drag him out naked. They arrested his wife and brother, too, though there was no reason to suspect them of anything. They were just grabbing everybody and keeping them in custody with no specified charges."

Dave's hands went cold, thinking of Hannah, Daisy, Jack,

Jen and Cliff.

"Here's just one of the kickers. When the wife and brother were released after a few days, they immediately lost their jobs."

"What happened to Raiman?"

"He was detained and interrogated for almost half a year in England. They got nothing out of him. The FBI ratcheted up the pressure by having him extradited to the U.S., so he was separated from his home, his family, and his friends. They claimed that he was the flight trainer for the guy who crashed into the Pentagon and that he had used a false name on the guy's application for a visa to enter the U.S."

"That's illegal, though."

"It would have been if it was true. But the visa application was never produced as evidence. The U.S. Government claimed it was a fact, but no one ever saw the actual document."

"Didn't they have to produce it for a judge to review?"

"Maybe. But here's the draconian thing. And I keep telling you this, Dave, because it's what Yusuf and you may be up against very soon. Under the new laws, the government doesn't have to show evidence to the accused's defense team. No one outside the government gets a chance to see anything to verify whether it's real or forged or to check its provenance."

Dave realized his breath had become shallow. "So did they bury this guy, Raiman?"

"Very nearly. By the time his case came to trial here in the U.S., the charges against him were stacked up like cord wood. They claimed they'd found his name on a document in the hijacker's rental vehicle left at Dulles Airport. They insisted they found a video on his computer showing him celebrating and bragging about his role in the attack. And supposedly they had phone records proving he had close connections with four of the other hijackers."

"You're saying they did bury him." He was quiet for a moment. "Is all this that you're telling me supposed to be encouraging somehow?"

"In a way, yes. Because—here's the thing—in Raiman's case, the U.S. judge insisted that the government produce the evidence, in open court, and the government refused to do it. The only flimsy little piece of paper they showed up at the trial with was Raiman's application for his pilot's license. They claimed he had lied on it by not stating that he'd had a minor knee surgery after a tennis accident. So *clearly*," Carl said, his voice full of sarcasm, "that proved he was a conspirator in the 9/11 attacks.

"And get this. The video footage of him celebrating with one of the conspirators? Turned out to be footage of him and a cousin celebrating at some family event, like a birthday party."

Dave stared. "And…?"

"The judge was probably enraged. Or maybe he held back from demanding the government explain why it brought such trumped-up, bullshit charges to his court. The bottom line was, he slapped a fine on Raiman, took his U.S. passport away, I guess he had to do something to show he was a good, so-called patriot, and sent the poor bastard home to London."

"With his life lying around him in shreds."

"You can't focus on that."

"Right. Thanks. There's an international round-up going on, and innocent people are being dragged into it. I'm trying not to get sick in your waste basket."

"I won't tell you to try to relax because I'm sure you can't. But I will tell you to keep as low a profile as possible."

"Lower than having no social contacts? Lower than hiding out in our home, waiting for Agent Murphy to show up with a swat team or another warrant and go through our underwear drawers?"

Carl stood and went to a credenza, where he poured water from a pitcher into a glass, which he handed to Dave.

"I'm not saying that. Live your life. Don't hide yourselves away. That makes you look guilty. But by keeping a low profile, I mean don't make any major purchases, like big, new vehicles or a vacation home. The government will have the IRS all over you to trace where the money came from. And don't go on any trips, especially not out of the country."

"I already told you. The cruise is dead."

"Now let's go back over Murphy's surprise visit. Tell me every detail. I want to see if any laws were broken or if any of your rights were violated."

"Would it even matter if they were? It feels like our lives are being violated and the government can do whatever the hell it wants to harass or destroy us."

"You've got friends and family and good business connects. Lean into them. So, tell me the whole story again."

*

Jen tapped lightly on Dave's door as she opened it, and when she stepped inside his office, he knew by her expression something big was on her mind.

"Murphy didn't show up at your house, did he?"

"No, thank God. I think Cliff might have lost it. I keep thinking about what a shock it must have been for you and Hannah last week."

"You look like you have some big news."

"No, and yes. Carter Gas and Petroleum requested that we

send all their files to their new accounting firm in Albany."

Dave nodded. "I was expecting that. The other firm can handle aspects of Carter's taxes that I'm not experienced in. Sorry to see them go, though. Good people. What else?"

Jen held up three more pink phone message sheets. "Three others phoned this morning as soon as I was at the door. Joe Howard called, Lester Appliance called, and the Marina called." She hesitated.

"I think I know what you're going to say. Just tell me."

"All three said they're moving their accounting business to other firms and can we transfer files immediately."

Dave winced.

"Joe Howard said he hopes there's no hard feelings and he wishes you luck."

"A friendly smile as he sticks the knife in."

Jen looked angry. "That totally unnecessary swat, the leaked story to the media, interviewing your acquaintances—I can't help but believe it's all meant to put a ridiculous amount of pressure on you."

Dave looked at the little brass clock in the corner of his desk. 9.07. The day had just started and his head was starting to pound.

"It's working. I don't have anything else to tell them. There's no information to give them. But if they just want to crush me, they're doing a good job."

"You didn't do anything wrong."

"I don't think that matters."

*

Hannah held out the phone receiver.

"It's your dad."

Dave hesitated. "Tell him I'm in the middle of something important and I'll call him back."

She gave him what he called *one of those looks*. "You can't keep what's happening from him forever. And it's not fair. You should have called him before now."

She was right. Any illusion that this mess would just blow over had vanished. He sucked in air and took the receiver.

"Hey, Pop. How's Florida? How's your golf handicap?"

"Son, you need to tell me what the hell's going on. A couple of my 'snowbird' friends just arrived from Saratoga for the winter and gave me an earful. Is any of it true?"

"Pop, I'm sorry you had to hear it from your friends. Listen, I'm cooperating in every way with the investigation into Yusuf Abdullah. Giving them everything they ask for. And I have a good lawyer."

"How are Hannah and Daisy?"

"I'm lucky to have two strong women in my life."

"Look, Dave, I'm ready to jump in my Buick, drive to Washington, and give someone hell. Just give me a name."

The thought of his father, at ninety years old and with his impaired vision, behind the wheel at all was daunting.

"My lawyer is getting the name of the U.S. Attorney who's the head of this. But I'm not giving it to you."

His father's voice softened. "What I called for is to say, son, you're a good man and everyone knows it. Everyone. You've spent decades building a successful business, and the reason you're successful is because you're honest and a hard worker. You're everything a good businessman should be. You and Hannah are a credit to your community. And…" The phone went silent.

Dave waited. "Pop, are you still there?"

Another moment of silence.

His father had choked up. "And you're everything a good son should be. I believe in you completely, David. I'll be here for you in any way I can, Hannah and Daisy, too."

Dave's throat tightened and he couldn't respond.

His father's tone switched to anger. "Now fight this every way you can."

"I will," Dave said.

"I know our country has to fight terrorism, and I want them to catch every murdering terrorist they can before they kill more innocent Americans. But you're a good man. The kind of son any father would be proud of."

When Hannah walked back into the room minutes later, she found Dave seated at the table. His face was in his hands and his shoulders were shaking. She had never seen him shed tears like this before.

Gently, she laid a hand on his shoulder.

"We'll get through this."

He had no words to respond.

*

Just before bed, walking Frankie along the quiet street, Dave kept hearing his father's last comment.

"But while they're fighting terrorists, the government can't be allowed to grind innocent Americans to powder in the process."

Frankie began to bark, and Dave looked across the street to see Alex Hartford, his neighbor and tennis buddy from back in the day, walking his golden retriever.

"Nice night," Dave called out.

Alex did not even glance over at him and picked up his pace without responding.

"... You're a good man and everyone knows it."

He watched Alex's form recede down the sidewalk, and thought of the clients that were cancelling their business with him. How many others were about to pull the plug?

Not everyone, Pop. Not by a long shot.

*

Dave stared at Carl King, wondering why part of his mind could still not believe what was happening to him.

"So, what you're telling me is that I can't even send a letter to my own clients, explaining my situation without passing it by a U.S. Attorney?"

"Let me put it this way: they're watching you so closely that you can't take a piss without permission."

"But these are clients I've had for years, and a number of them are bailing out on me. How am I supposed to save my business?"

"The government doesn't care about that. Dave, if you draft a letter, I'll send it to the U.S. Attorney for his approval or redrafting."

"Redrafting. So, he can put words in my mouth, so to speak, and I'm supposed to be okay with that. What if I don't like his version of the letter."

Carl leaned across the desk. "I get that you're under pressure, but you… we… have to play along to some degree. We have to get the guy's approval and whatever he sends back, you have to send it out to your clients. Otherwise, it looks like you're concealing the truth and resisting the government's efforts to fight the terrorists."

"So, they've got my… hand in a vise."

"Along with some more tender parts."

Dave stared at his shoe tops, thinking that just months ago all he'd had to concern himself with was seeing that Daisy had a beautiful wedding and planning a cruise with Hannah. The usual stuff of a normal, everyday life. Now he was stuck in a nightmare that wouldn't let him wake up.

*

Jen stuck her head in his office door.

"Are you okay?"

Dave was staring at his computer, with its blinking cursor. His hands were not on the keys.

"Sure. Let's say I am. Why?"

"Because line one is blinking on your phone and you didn't pick up, and you're not answering my page."

He kept staring at the cursor on the blank screen.

"Who is it?"

"Les Thackery."

Dave's stomach knotted. Les was a long-time client, who owned three huge furniture showrooms and was a partner in one of the large marinas on Lake George.

"What's he want?"

"He wants to talk to you, of course."

"What about?"

"You know I don't ask. Just pick up." She added, "He sounds friendly."

Friendly. Sure. Then the axe comes down on my neck.

"Hey, Les," Dave tried to sound relaxed. He almost said,

"How's business?" but veered in another direction. "How's the family?"

"They're fine. The question is, how are you and your family? Louise and I are concerned."

Dave stumbled for an answer, thinking, *What if my phone is tapped?* He didn't want to sound too confident and didn't want to say too much, and realized then how deeply the government's hooks had dug into his mind.

"We're not doing great, to be honest. But," he thought to add, "since Hannah and I know I haven't done anything wrong, we're hopeful that the justice system will do its job and I'll be shown to be innocent."

If anyone was listening, he hoped he'd punched them in the jaw—not too hard, but with a clear, consistent message.

"I'm calling to see if you're up for a round of golf."

That was unexpected. He and Les had played regularly a few years back, but they'd both become busy and fallen out of the habit.

"I'm rusty, and I think my clubs are covered in cobwebs. You'd probably bury me."

"Good, because we're going to bet twenty dollars on the game, and I don't plan to lose. I was hoping you'd agree and I've booked a tee-off time for eight on Saturday."

Dave relaxed a little. "In two days? That doesn't give me enough time to loosen up my right shoulder."

"Come on, old man. See you on the links."

*

"You weren't kidding about your shoulder," said Les on the green of the fifth hole. "I see you wincing when you drive."

A red-tailed hawk was perched in a pine tree next to the green, eyeing the fairway for small creatures unaware, and a light breeze brought the scent of fresh water from the small lake nearby.

Dave almost felt good.

"Yeah," he replied. "Play football when you're young; live with pain the rest of your life."

"At least it wasn't a traumatic head injury. Those poor guys start to lose it in their forties and fifties."

"I don't know. I feel like I've been stomped and kicked in the head." It just came out. He hadn't meant to allude in any way to the investigation.

Les was taking a putter out of his bag and paused.

"Louise and I are on your side, Dave. We want you and Hannah to know that. Honestly, that's why I invited you to play today. Show of friendship and solidarity."

Dave took in a deep breath of the fresh air, realizing he'd been tense all morning, waiting for a shoe to drop. Hannah's words came back and became his own.

"He's not going to invite you to play golf to tell you he's dropping your services."

"It's just, you know, what I've come to expect."

"You're a good friend, Les. Thanks. Thank Louise for us, too."

"She's planning on asking Hannah out to lunch. Probably calling her today."

Dave watched Les take the putter out of his bag, then hesitated again.

"It's gotta be terrible to have the government accuse you of hiding something from them. I know. I was audited that one time, remember? I felt like a criminal. You start to think of all the little things you might have done wrong, accidentally or just because, in a moment of weakness or indiscretion, you slipped some little thing by."

"Do I remember? We went through every entry in your books for years to clear you."

Les was addressing the ball, head down.

"Yeah, it's those little indiscretions that can get you, though. The kind you barely even remember you committed. Do you ever worry about those?"

Dave was about to say no, but another thought slammed him, along with a rush of paranoia.

"Are you… thinking I might admit to something? Because you're an old friend and you think I might come clean with you? divulge something?" His face was growing red with anger.

Les straightened up.

"Seriously? Do you think I invited you out today to see if I could get you to 'fess up to something?"

"Sorry, but given what I'm facing…" His voice trailed off.

"Dave, I'm a friend. This is not part of a set-up. I'm not wearing a wire. Do you want me to strip down to my shorts and let you check me for a recording device?"

"Good lord, please don't."

The tense mood broke.

"I only know that when I was under the government interrogation lights, I could hardly sleep nights. I kept imagining that someone at one of my showrooms or at the marina—or *I*—would enter some figures wrong, and it would look like I was trying to pull a fast one.

"Then I woke up one night, remembering I'd pulled some cash from the business—not a lot, maybe two hundred dollars—to pay for a personal expense. I couldn't recall if I reimbursed the business, which I'd fully intended to do. Always do. And I pictured myself admitting to that and being screwed by the I.R.S. for one tiny misstep."

Dave was watching him closely. "I didn't know you were struggling like that at the time."

"See, that's the thing. I'm generally a hundred percent honest guy. But one little misstep, and your conscience nails you. That's the problem for really honest guys, like I know you are. Your conscience can tear you up. That's what I really wanted to know when I asked if you'd committed any indiscretions. How badly are you struggling? I just didn't ask it the right way. Sorry, I threw you."

Dave relaxed. A little. He believed what Les was saying. He was also not going to let his guard down completely.

"It's all good. Let's play. You know I'm two strokes ahead already, right?"

Les addressed the ball again, then paused. Turning up the collar of his Polo shirt, he pretended to whisper into a hidden mic.

"Dave thinks he's going to win. And he just might."

*

After a break at the ninth hole, they walked to the tenth tee. A lone golfer was there ahead of them, loosening up with his driver before teeing off. He was wearing a red and blue striped shirt with white stars in a blue field across the shoulders.

"Ken Avery," Dave called to him. "I guess they'll let anyone play on this course."

The golfer barely glanced over his shoulder, and kept practicing.

Supposing he didn't hear, Dave repeated, "I said, I guess

they'll let anyone play."

This time, Avery turned around. His expression was somewhere between blank and disgusted.

"Yeah, it looks like it."

Les stuck out his hand, which Avery ignored.

"Looks like they'll even let guys play here who betray their country."

Les's expression went cold and he stepped up to Avery until they were almost chest-to-chest.

"Whatever happened to 'innocent until proven guilty'? If you knew Dave at all, the way I do after working with him and his firm for decades, you'd never say a stupid thing like that."

The color went up Avery's neck.

"Why do I care what you have to say? You wouldn't be seen with this guy if you were any kind of a patriot."

Dave felt kicked in the stomach.

"*Patriot?*" Les shot back at Avery. "You guys kill me. You toss around that word like you know what it really means and like you have some exclusive right to it."

"We need more patriots in this country," Avery came back, with an angry edge to his voice. "Anyone who doesn't love this country or who won't stand up for it against 'enemies foreign and domestic' should get the hell out."

Les did not back down. "That's a nice jingoism. 'Love this country or get out.' You right-wingers are like a bunch of parrots."

"I know where there's smoke, there's usually fire."

"*Sometimes*, but not always. Did it ever occur to you that you're being manipulated to support certain causes the government wants you to get behind without questioning? Right now, it looks to me like the government seems to be on a bender to hang anyone they point a finger at. And it doesn't matter to guys like you, who hand your brain over and let them do the thinking for you."

Avery looked as if the veins in his neck would burst.

"Get out of my face."

*

Hannah looked happier than he'd seen her in days when Dave walked in the door.

"How was the game? How's your shoulder?"

Dave went to the refrigerator and filled a glass with cold water from the dispenser. He had a headache.

"It was fine. My shoulder's… stiff, but it'll be fine."

"You should ice it. What am I saying? I know you won't. By the way, Les's wife, Louise, called. She wants to have lunch and suggested the club by the marina. I asked if we could meet someplace quieter, like that little café by the bike shop in Lake George."

"Not like you to pass up the chance for lunch at the club."

"I—." Hannah's smile left as she stopped, searching for the words. "I just feel so exposed and vulnerable in public now. *Damn,* what these people are doing to you. To *us*. The truth is, I'm afraid someone will come up to me in public and say something terrible that I don't need to hear. Do you know what I mean?"

Dave opened the plastic bottle of headache tablets and shook out two, then a third, into his palm.

"Yeah. I do."

"Why is a supposedly democratic nation doing this railroading to you?"

He swallowed the tablets with a big gulp of water.

Because a lot of its citizens need an enemy to hate and target. And if they can't find the real enemy, they'll find scapegoats.

"It's like they don't care whose life they ruin."

Dave remained silent. He decided he would not tell her about the run-in with Ken Avery—*That flag-waving jerk.*

Hannah stood at the window, staring out at the sky.

"This isn't the America I was raised to believe in and love."

Dave was at a loss for words.

"You'd give your life for this country. So, would I? Don't they get that?"

If they do, I'm afraid they don't give a damn.

Chapter 9

"Whatever you do, don't let him get to you. They want to get under your skin and make you angry. When you lose control, you're liable to slip up and make the kind of statements they're hoping you'll come out with."

Dave looked at the clock on Carl's desk at 9.57 and then across the desk at his lawyer. "I'm not hiding anything. There isn't anything I can say that they can use against me."

Carl shook his head. "If they get you angry enough to start shouting things against them, the government or anything at all like that, they'll use it to pressure you and repeat it in open court."

Dave sat back, like he'd been punched. "Open court. You think I'll be put on trial?"

"That could depend on what you say today."

At exactly ten a.m., there was a knock at Carl's office door.

Thanks, a hell of a lot, Carl. No pressure.

Agent Murphy entered along with two men in dark suits. One carried a small recorder, which he set down on Carl's desk next to Dave.

"Let's get started," said Agent Murphy.

Yeah. Started. I feel like I'm finished.

Murphy settled into a chair. "Before we begin, you need to know this. Willful blindness is not a defense."

Dave opened his mouth to reply, and Carl cut him off.

"What does that mean, 'willful blindness'?"

The man who had placed the recorder next to Dave pressed

a button.

"Mr. Mattson here cannot claim that Mr. Abdullah's foundation was not legally related to the entity that filed the application for non-profit status before or at the time the application was filed. Making such a claim that there were two separate entities and he, Mr. Mattson, was only related to the one *not* making the application—that is considered 'willful blindness."

Carl intervened. "Why are you saying 'willful'?"

"As an agent of Dr. Abdullah filing the application, Mr. Mattson was responsible for knowing all entities connected to and benefiting from the application's approval. Beyond that, it is reasonably assumed that he had to know that organizations created by Dr. Abdullah were related and would use the non-profit status to benefit all his work, but he chose to ignore that fact."

Dave stared at him.

Murphy looked at him without expression. "That means you can be subject to possible criminal charges."

Dave's gut twisted into a knot.

Murphy handed him a letter.

"This is from the non-CPA accountant, and it was sent to you at the time Dr. Abdullah fired that person and hired you to complete the application. Please take your time and read it."

Dave scrutinized the lines carefully, and the more he read, the more he felt himself growing warm around the collar. The letter revealed more about the situation and problems related to it than he remembered. The main revelation was that the accountant had been asked to do things far beyond what was necessary to fill out the form things that amounted to bending the truth.

In his mind's-eye, he saw himself dodging Yusuf, feeling pressured by Daisy's imminent wedding, trying to get through the pressures of tax season, and ignoring what should have been clear warnings not to proceed. All, to get Yusuf off his back.

There were sounds from Carl's outer office, and someone shoved open the door.

"My husband is in there and *I am going in*."

The agent, who had been guarding the door, looked at Murphy, who nodded.

When Hannah was seated beside Dave, holding his hand, Murphy raised an eyebrow.

"What's your response to this letter?—which we got from your files and have shown to the U.S. Attorney prosecuting this case. Clearly, it indicates you knew there were irregularities with the application and that the non-CPA was being pressured to fill in whatever was necessary to obtain the U.S. Postal Service's approval."

"I…" Dave stammered. He wanted to kick himself. Hard.

"Don't respond to that," Carl intervened again.

Murphy continued to come at Dave from different angles.

"Did you think making your assistant work on the application would somehow protect you from possible prosecution? Before you answer, you should know that Mary has already told us, on record, that she went to you several times for help and you advised her on how to handle the form.

"Did you think your claim—let me read from my notes, 'It was tax season and I was overwhelmed'—did you think that would form a useful defense? Because you also indicated again, let me read, 'Yes, I read the letter from Dr. Abdullah's previous accountant.'"

"Or this? 'Mary was fairly new, and I believed that having

her handle this application would be good training. So, I wasn't as attentive to the details as I might have been.'"

At each onslaught, Carl stepped in. "Don't respond."

Hannah was squeezing Dave's hand. He could feel her trembling.

Agent Murphy had clearly had enough.

"It's obvious you think that claiming ignorance and saying nothing now is going to help you. I can assure you, it won't. Mr. Mattson, Mrs. Mattson, let me give you some advice."

They stared at him.

"Life as you know it is over."

Hannah bristled. "That's not advice; that's a threat."

Dave squeezed her hand hard, to stop her from saying more. He was shifting in his seat, feeling nauseous.

"Not a threat. Advisement," said Murphy, standing and preparing to leave. "Here's the advice. Hire a good criminal lawyer. You're going to need one."

As he walked out the door, Agent Murphy added. "And when you've hired someone, have them contact U.S. Attorney Emanuel Rodriguez. He's been assigned to this case now. He'll listen to today's interview and I can guarantee he'll want to conduct a follow-up."

When he was gone, Hannah was shaking with anger.

"How can they do this?"

Carl was silent for a moment.

"They're with the government. They can do whatever the hell they want."

"Mattson is refusing to cooperate," said Murphy, opening the conversation with Rodriguez.

"Is this your report?" the U.S. Attorney responded, picking up the file on his desk. "Does it detail everything about the interview? Mattson's responses, his facial expressions and body language?"

"Yes, it does."

Rodriguez studied Agent Murphy. "You're confident about proceeding with this case? You've questioned and observed him enough and can make strong, unequivocal statements in court?"

Agent Murphy hesitated.

"I don't like that you're not answering."

"Mattson is a small fish, at best."

"Connected to the bigger one we're after."

"This will change Mattson's life forever." His statement, *"Life as you know it is over,"* has begun to haunt him. Is this why he had become a federal agent?

Rodriguez' voice took on an edge. He pointed to a whiteboard behind him, with news articles taped to it.

"In Sri Lanka, Islamic terrorists slaughtered hundreds of people in Christian churches. These people were praying, and they were cut down by automatic weapons. More have been killed on the streets."

He pointed to the second and third articles.

"In Montreal, a van loaded with Muslim extremists jumped a curb and plowed through people enjoying a Saturday afternoon and eating at a sidewalk café. Dozens were injured or killed."

"In Paris, more deadly assaults by extremists."

Murphy nodded and said nothing.

"Agent Murphy, every single day, U.S. and foreign intelligence services pick up or are informed of a dozen more threats to innocent civilians and government or military targets here at home and abroad. Tell me you're not getting too soft for this war on terror."

"Life as you know it is over." A statement of truth, no matter

how anyone cut it or how the Mattsons took it.

"No," he responded. "Life as we've known it is over for everyone."

Rodriguez nodded. "And there are bound to be casualties none of us are very happy about. But that's what happens in war, isn't it? There are casualties."

Murphy was silent.

"You don't want to be one of those casualties, do you?" said Rodriguez.

Murphy crushed the small flicker of remorse. *Mattson was aiding and abetting. Period. He needs to be nailed. Just do your job,* he told himself. *Don't overthink it.*

*

Don't think, Dave repeated over and over as he walked to work. He needed the long walk and he needed to keep his mind from spinning out all the dark possibilities.

Halfway to the office, he made a detour.

Evelyn was sitting beside a sunny window, eyes closed, looking more frail than he had ever seen her. The sun highlighted the old, blue-veined skin on her hands.

"How's my girlfriend?"

Her eyes came open.

"Girlfriend, is it? If that's the case, let's go to my room and have at it."

He laughed.

"That's what I want to see—you laughing at this whole mess."

He dropped down heavily into the chair next to hers.

"What 'whole mess' are you talking about?"

She almost snorted.

"Please. Hannah came by to see me."

"I don't want this visit to be all about us. About me. I came to see how you're getting along."

"I have a great-nephew who can't wait for me to fall down a flight of stairs, hoping he's named in my will, which he isn't. He's lazy. Albert, who you met last time, was carried out by the boots two days ago. I'd rather talk legal strategy with you. I know it's an oxymoron, but do you have a good lawyer?"

"Yes. I've just had to hire a criminal lawyer. But I'm guessing Hannah already told you that. It's mortifying. Never in a million years did I think I'd have to hire someone to defend me."

Evelyn took his hand.

"Look me in the eye, Dave."

He focused on her face, seeing how her lips pursed and her eyes narrowed in a defiant expression.

"Do not roll over. All I hear on TV is 'the war on terror,' 'the war on terror,' and I don't suppose anyone wants to be blown up on a subway or gunned down shopping. But."

She leaned forward. "Do not let the government terrorize *you*."

He smiled weakly.

"There. That's what I mean. You look defeated. They're getting inside your head."

"How can you fight them, Ev? They're the government."

"What I'm saying is you can't let them or this whole set-up crush your spirit. This is the first line of battle. Stay strong."

He nodded.

Easy to say, hard to do.

She was watching him closely.

"Don't pretend you agree with me while you're disagreeing on the inside. I can see through you."

"Dear God, you're a better interrogator than the guy they keep throwing at me. And he's a pit bull."

"I would love to interrogate your government, goon. I'd have him gibbering in a corner in sixty seconds flat."

Dave broke into a wide grin and laughed. A hearty laugh.

Evelyn grinned.

"I see that my work here is done. Now, I hope you won't think me rude, Dave, but I need to get these old bones over to the *Mah Jong* game that's about to start in the other parlor. I'm trying to get those timid old biddies to place cash bets, and today I may browbeat them into it."

*

The small fire Evelyn had stoked within him lasted most of the way to the office.

On the street outside, a black sedan with government plates eroded the little bit of good mood he'd taken away with him.

Inside, Jen was trying to hide a look of concern, but he saw through it.

"What's up?"

"It's been two weeks since the letter went out."

The letter was the one the U.S. Attorney had reviewed and amended. It allowed him to tell his clients that he was involved in a situation which, he believed, would not affect his business "now or in the future." It said he was available to serve their accounting needs and looked forward to continuing to work together.

"Well..." Jen said slowly. "No one has replied so far."

In the silence, they could hear the hum of the overhead light. Evelyn's voice came back.

"You can't let them crush your spirit. This is the first line of battle. Stay strong."

"But no one has written or called to say they're taking their business elsewhere, have they?"

Jen's face brightened a little.

"No."

"Good. Let's hold onto that today."

Alone in his office, he hoped he could live up to that statement. Despite Evelyn's words and his forced, surface bravado, he felt shut down and numb.

Until the afternoon, he happened to glance out the window, which triggered the memory of the swat team surrounding him, and felt like some new, terrible thing was about to happen.

*

The dark figure had both hands around his throat, and it was becoming harder and harder to breathe. Someone was shaking him.

"David, wake up. *David.*"

He almost took a swing at the person shaking him but caught himself in time, aware that it was Hannah.

As he sat up in the dark, heart racing, he caught his breath.

Hannah turned on the bedside light, her face ashen. "Are you all right? Are you having chest pains?"

He blinked, dazed, his breathing rapid. "No. I just... can't breathe right."

"I'm calling an ambulance," Hannah said, reaching for her cell phone on the nightstand.

He laid his hand on her arm. "No. I don't need it."

She pulled her arm away. "I'm not putting up with your 'I don't need a doctor' bullshit. If you don't want an ambulance, I'm driving you to the ER."

Dave had trouble focusing. His breath was shallow and he was lightheaded. *Please, God, not a stroke.*

Nothing was numb; he could move his limbs, and his vision was okay. "I think I'm just fine," he said, testing his ability to speak.

Hannah had quickly dressed, and she threw his jeans and a shirt at him.

"Get in the car. Or I'll call the ambulance and the police, and I'll tell them you're having some kind of attack and you're not cooperative. You'll hate it if they slap you on a gurney and restrain you."

*

The ER doctor had finished checking his vitals and asking a host of questions, testing his cognitive abilities.

"Your blood pressure is slightly above where it should be, but," he tried to lighten the mood by tapping Dave's stomach, "carrying these extra pounds, along with your age, can be the cause of that. Everything else checks out as normal, physically speaking."

"Normal?" Hannah shot back. "He couldn't breathe."

"I said physically speaking. In my experience, Mr. Mattson, I suspect you were having a panic attack. Is anything going on in your life that might trigger an event like that?"

Dave and Hannah looked at each other.

"Do you watch the news?"

"As little as possible. Why?"

The wall clock said 3.19 a.m. Dave was exhausted and Hannah looked spent.

"Skip it," Dave replied. "What do I do about this, if it's what you say—a panic attack? It was pretty bad."

"I thought he was choking to death, the way he was gasping," Hannah added.

"I'm sending you home with scrips for two anti-anxiety meds. One works on a long-term basis, in case there are stressors in your life that are factors here. The other is for immediate intervention, if you have another episode where you can't breathe. It will calm you down fast."

Dave was shaken.

"So, this could happen again."

The doctor was noncommittal. "Sometimes these events happen just once and never again. Sometimes, they return. You said this is a first and you hinted that there's something big going on in your life. I want you to be prepared, is all."

At home, Dave crawled into bed and tried to settle. In a few minutes, he realized Hannah had not come into the bedroom.

He found her out in the front room, with her face in her hands. She was shaking.

When she looked up, she said, "We have to be stronger than this or they've already won."

*

Arriving early at the office the next morning, he sat alone in the quiet. He doubted that coffee was going to help, and the doctor had told him to avoid caffeine.

The events of last night made it clear that he now had one

main job, and that was to survive and try to hold on to what was left of his professional and personal life. Yet he felt as if he was standing on a foundation made of straw.

Reaching inside in search of strength, he leaned on the words his father had said to him.

"Listen carefully, David. No matter how this ends up, I'll be there for you. I am very proud of you, and nothing these bastards do or say will change that."

That brought back a measure of peace—small, but a place to stand within himself.

Beyond that, he forced himself not to think of what the government could do to him.

*

Alone in his office, Agent Murphy went back through all his notes. Rodriguez' caution or was it a personal warning, kept playing in his head.

"You don't want to be one of the casualties, do you?"

He had worked too hard for years and was a good agent. No, a great one. He would not let one case sidetrack or wreck his career. Mattson had played footsie with a possible enemy. No, an enemy.

Closing his notepad, he focused on one goal. There was always dirt to find or even just something that looked like dirt. He would find it.

In this war, if it was Dave Mattson or him, there was no contest. The big loser here would be Mattson.

Chapter 10

"Have you read the Albany paper this morning?" Daisy's voice on the phone was strained.

"Is my name in it?" It was only six fifteen a.m., and Dave stared out the back window, feeling tense already.

"No, but you need to read it."

Hannah came into the kitchen with the paper she had retrieved from the front porch.

She dropped it on the table in front of him and pointed at the headline.

"I'll call you back," Dave said to Daisy. "I think my death warrant is here."

"Dad, stop."

"I'll call you back. Love you."

There was a front-page story about Yusuf. Dave scanned it quickly, and saw that he had been picked up by agents along with several others who worked at the new Bread for Children Foundation offices and taken to the federal justice center in Albany. After lengthy questioning, several were let go, but Yusuf and the office manager of the foundation had been arrested.

"Oh, dear lord," said Hannah, starting to read over his shoulder out loud.

"According to sources, Yusuf Abdullah was on his way to the office when his car was cut off by federal agents. He was removed from it, placed in handcuffs, and taken to the Justice Center."

"His wife was at home," Hannah continued, "and a group of federal agents served her with a search warrant and placed her in custody. She was not arrested and was released after hours of questioning. The home search did not find anything incriminating, though computers were seized."

Dave felt the pulse in his neck.

"All of this is scary as hell, but they seized their computers. That's terrifying."

Hannah stared. "Being dragged out of your car and home isn't bad enough?"

"Of course. But what are the chances that while the authorities are examining the Abdullah's computers, they'll *find* some damaging information?"

"'Find' as in 'plant' evidence against them? Dave, that's criminal."

"What if they've determined they don't really have much of a case against Yusuf? After all the noise they've generated around this case, the government has to come up with something."

"But they arrested him and his office manager. Doesn't that mean they have something on them?"

"Not under the rules of the Patriot Act, it doesn't. The feds can detain someone for as long as they want while they're *looking* for the evidence to hold them."

In twenty minutes, there was a knock at the front door, and Dave and Hannah were startled. Before they could get up to answer, they heard the door open and footsteps coming through the front room toward the kitchen.

Daisy appeared, followed by Jack.

"*What's wrong?*" Daisy said, seeing her parents' faces.

Dave and Hannah both let out their breath.

"We thought you were someone else."

Jack stuck out his hand to Dave. "We both took the morning off because we wanted to come over here and tell you in person that we're with you all the way, one hundred percent, whatever happens."

Dave gripped his son-in-law's hand while Hannah threw her arms around Daisy.

"You have no idea how much this means," Dave said, looking Jack in the eye, "because right now it seems like anything could happen. And I mean anything."

*

Carl King paced his law office's small conference room.

"Is this why we're meeting, so you could give me this information?" Dave asked. The visit from Daisy and Jack had helped to steady him, but Carl's urgent call later was troubling.

"I asked you here because it's safe to talk in this room. I've had it scanned for listening devices. You should know what's happening behind closed doors at the Justice Center. Someone inside passed on information."

"Who?"

"You only need to know that they're reliable. They said that Dr. Abdullah was taken into an interrogation room early in the morning and questioned for hours. He wasn't given water or a break to use the men's room. They wouldn't tell him anything about his wife; other than that, she was in custody and was giving them information. Which she wasn't. And he asked repeatedly to call his lawyer, but they denied him the right to do that until late that evening."

"That's terrible," Dave responded. "Are you warning me

that they could do this to me?" and the thought hit him, "and Hannah?"

Carl stopped pacing.

"No, but that is possible. Sorry. I called you here to tell you that your name came up during Abdullah's interrogation. In fact, he brought it up."

Dave's throat went dry.

"What did he say?"

"This is where my source is sketchy. He knows your name was mentioned, but he doesn't know if what Abdullah said puts you in a good light or a bad light."

Suddenly, Dave felt like he was walking on sinking sand.

"I'm telling you this because the government is really upping their game in this case. If they have information your lawyer doesn't have, that makes it harder to defend you. So..." He looked Dave directly in the eye.

"Look, there's nothing I'm not telling you guys. No surprises from me."

Carl began pacing again.

"I didn't think so. But they've got Abdullah's computers and whatever he just told them, including using your name. What concerns me are the surprises the government can spring on us."

*

Jen looked up when Dave entered his office, and handed him the *New York Times*. She pointed to an article that began at the bottom of page one, where he read,

"*U.S. Attorney General John Ashcroft made these remarks in a press conference this morning: 'Not only will terrorists be aggressively pursued and punished to the full extent of the law, but any and all people who supported their causes would be prosecuted, as well."*

Jen was staring at him when he finished reading.

"These are really big guns aimed at you, Dave."

Thanks for that, he almost said, but didn't. He knew she was only bringing this up out of genuine concern that he be well prepared.

"I just hope Carl King is the right guy to be defending you."

Carl's own final words were still sounding in Dave's head.

"What I've got in my legal arsenal is very likely a lot less than the U.S. Attorney's inventory of weapons. It's going to seem like I have a slingshot and the U.S. Attorney has cannons and tanks. Those guys are fighting on a level that's way above any of us common defense lawyers. The thing is, we're the American citizens' only front line of defense against them."

Great. So, the odds are stacked against me all around. What's the point of even trying to fight this?

"Dave—?"

Jen's voice brought him back to the present moment.

"I said, When's your next meeting with King?"

"He wants me to hire another lawyer. I don't know if he's giving up on me or he really wants someone better equipped to handle my case."

*

And there it was, coming online. Dave Mattson's home laptop.

Agent Murphy stood beside the counter-terrorism tech and watched as the first files opened. Golf tips. Natural remedies for stress. Articles by massage therapists specializing in stress relief.

Surveillance told him Mattson had just left his office, and

clearly Hannah Mattson was now home from work, looking at articles she'd downloaded.

"This can't be what you're looking for," said the tech.

"Can you tap into his saved files, emails, everything in this?"

"Just give me search words."

"I'll take it from here."

The tech balked. "You're asking me to turn over my computer so you can search his? Shouldn't you get a warrant and seize it? This kind of remote incursion is crossing a line, isn't it? You could be accused later of planting information in the suspect's files."

"Let me worry about that," said Murphy.

*

All the way home, weighed down by a deep-level exhaustion he'd never felt before, one thought kept circling in his head.

If I could just lay down somewhere and quit...

Slipping in the front door quietly, he made his way down the hall to his office before facing Hannah. She would read him instantly and he didn't want her to know how he felt right now. It would only bring her further down than she was already.

Alone, he couldn't fight the dark thoughts.

The laptop's cursor was blinking. Hannah had been in here again, probably doing medical research, determined to get him to take the medications the ER doc had prescribed. He tried to turn off the computer, but it wouldn't shut down.

I need to get out here to work on this dinosaur, he thought briefly, but it was the least of his worries.

I'm sunk.

They'll send me to prison.

What am I looking at—ten years? twenty?

If there was a bottom to hit that was lower than this, he didn't want to find it.

Evelyn's voice came back. *"Fight this!"*

Daisy and Jack's faces were there, loving and supportive.

If there was any strength to be found to fight this, he didn't know where it would come from. Certainly not from within himself.

Tapping at his office door roused him.

"Yeah," he said, his voice sounding weak.

Hannah opened the door and stepped into the room.

"Someone's here. You need to come out of hiding."

"How'd you know I was in here?"

She let out a long sigh and shook her head. "*A*, how long have we been married? And *B*, you're not exactly Tinker Bell when you try to sneak in the front door."

"Who's out there? Please tell me it's not Agent Murphy."

"It's not Agent Murphy. There. Now, will you just come out here? You need this. *We* need this."

Seated in the front room were Alex Hartford and his wife, Kara. Alex stood when Dave walked in.

"We felt it was time we came by and told you how we feel about all that's going on with you."

Here it comes.

"What? You want us to sell the house and get out of the neighborhood, right—?

"*Dave*," Hannah interrupted. "Just listen."

"Good lord, no." Alex extended his hand for Dave to shake. "We came to tell you most of the neighborhood is behind you. We've all known you guys for years, and you're good people."

Kara said, frowning, "We've been concerned, watching the

news and reading about what's going on in this country. We think the government is going overboard with surveillance and going after people who turn out to be innocent."

"And in the meantime," Alex added, "they destroy people's reputations and lives."

Dave stared at him for a moment. "I'm surprised, Alex."

"Why?"

"A few nights ago, I saw you out walking your dog and I called out to you. You totally ignored me. I took that as a big 'Go to hell.'"

Alex looked shocked. "Dave, no way. Hey, when I'm out walking the dog, I have earbuds in and I'm listening to music on my iPod. It's so damn boring waiting for that dog to quit sniffing at everything and unload for the night."

Hannah laid her hand on Dave's arm.

"See, we both needed to hear this. Not everyone's against us. It just feels that way right now."

"You said most of the neighbors are on our side. I assume that means that some of them are not."

Alex shook his head. "That's people. Some jump to conclusions. You know, 'Where there's smoke, there must be fire.'"

Ken Avery had thrown that old chestnut at him.

Kara said, "Dave, he's talking about only two couples out of, what?—thirty or more in this neighborhood?"

"So, I guess you've all been talking."

"Of course," said Alex, "but the talk's all good, in your favor. I guess the government has blown its credibility too many times."

"You should hear Alex go on," said Kara, "about how the government lied about the Gulf of Tonkin and made up the story that Vietnamese gunboats had fired on American ships, using that to justify escalating the Vietnam War."

Alex nodded. "False flag events. Planted evidence. Coerced testimonies. There's too much evidence that they manipulate the information, trying to get us all to just knuckle under and believe them whenever they point the finger."

"And a lot of us," said Kara, "just don't buy every single thing the government tries to sell anymore."

When the Hartfords were gone, Hannah said, "Wasn't that worth coming out of hiding for? If you were feeling down, why were you hiding from *me*?"

"I didn't want to spread my contagion of bad feelings."

Hannah grabbed him by the shoulders and pulled him around to face her.

"Are we partners in everything or aren't we, David?"

"*David.* I guess I'm in trouble."

"Stop playing this off. Are we in this together? Totally. Or aren't we?"

Not long before, he had wondered where he'd find the strength to get through this nightmare. How he'd survive if the worst happened and the government buried him alive in a steel cage somewhere?

Now he had some ideas.

Chapter 11

"I can't figure out why this thing would behave like that, Dave," said Jack.

"Some neighbors showed up, and I forgot that it was giving me trouble. About an hour later, I came back into the office and the cursor was still blinking. It was on, but I couldn't do anything with it. Couldn't access files. Couldn't shut it down. Nothing."

"I can upload new programs and transfer all your files over, but it'll take me time. If it's the hard drive, though, you'll need to get someone with more skill than me to work on it. But let me try what I know first. Save you some bucks."

Daisy came into the office. "Can you work on it here? That way, you won't have to lug it."

"I'd rather take my time and do a thorough job. I'll bet this old thing hasn't been updated in a long time."

Hannah had followed Daisy into the office. "I've also pulled some boxes from the closet in your old room, honey. Stuff from way back in junior high. Your old books, dolls, CDs, and notes from old crushes."

"Help me load them in the car and I'll get them out of your hair."

Jack tapped the laptop. "Got a box for this? I can check it all out for you right away and get it back."

Dave went in search of a box big enough.

When he returned from the basement ten minutes later with an empty container, the laptop was gone.

Out in the driveway, Hannah and Daisy were talking quietly next to the cars. The trunk of Daisy's car was open and it was filled with boxes and large garment bags. Finally, she'd emptied the closet in her old room.

"Did you guys find a box?"

They hesitated.

"Where's Jack?"

"He went back in to look for you," Daisy replied.

Jack was waiting in the kitchen.

"I didn't want to say this in front of them." He nodded toward the women outside. "I've got a college buddy who went into cyber security. I'm going to have him check out your computer."

"Why? I haven't used it to do anything suspect."

"That's not what I'm concerned about."

*

Andrew Samson stood and leaned across the highly polished conference table to shake Dave's hand, nodding in greeting to Carl King at the same time.

"Andrew has been in criminal defense work for—what it is?—twenty or twenty-five years?" said Carl.

Dave was surprised. Samson looked to be maybe just forty years old, lean, athletic build, and good-looking. He could have been a model in men's health and sports magazines. In comparison, Carl looked like a guy who'd smoked too many cigars and eaten too many Philly cheesesteaks and couldn't tie his shoes without getting winded. Samson's sharper image was somehow reassuring and Dave realized that's what he was looking for here. Assurance.

Samson didn't smile and motioned for them to be seated.

So. All business. But does he really have the chops for this?

"I've reviewed all the notes Carl sent me and made first contact with the U.S. Attorney."

"And?" Carl prompted.

"Let's just say the sparring has begun. This guy's tough."

"What happened?"

"His opening salvo was to tell me, before I even asked, that the government doesn't have to show me any evidence they have in this case. I told him I was already aware of that, but that I would be well prepared for whatever they could present."

"Typical lawyer chest-bumping," Carl interjected.

Samson ignored him, folded his hands and looked Dave squarely in the face. "That's why you have to tell me absolutely everything. You can't hold back or hide anything. Not one phone call, email or secret computer file."

Dave sat back at that.

"What do you mean secret file? There aren't any."

"Rodriguez mentioned it two or three times, so I believe he thinks there are some."

"Dave just told you there aren't any."

Samson ignored him again, and looked irritated.

"Mr. Mattson can speak for himself here, I assume."

Fantastic. My own lawyers are locking horns.

Dave leaned forward and stared Samson in the eye.

"Like I just said, there aren't any. And I need to know that you believe me. Because it's the truth."

Samson drummed the tips of his fingers on the table.

"Rodriguez is either bluffing or trying to drive a wedge between us from the get-go. Or…"

Dave waited. "Or what."

"Or they've gotten to your computer."

"It's not even at my home anymore. And no one searched the files while they were still there."

"I don't mean 'gotten to it' in that way."

*

Agent Murphy stepped out the front door as Dave arrived home.

Hannah was behind him, her face grim.

"I have a warrant to seize and search your home computer, but it seems as though you've moved it."

"I didn't. The last time I saw it, it was sitting on my desk."

"Then who did remove it?"

Dave's mind flipped back to the scene. Jack had asked for a box. He'd gone to the basement. When he found the group again, all the boxes had been loaded in the car, the women were talking and Jack was inside.

"I have no idea. None." He suppressed a grin. "Are you sure your guys didn't take it?" He nodded at the two men standing beside Murphy. "Hannah, were you with them the whole time? Did these guys take my laptop out of the house?"

Murphy's face went bright red.

"You can play games with me here, Mr. Mattson. But when you're in court and under oath, you'll be compelled to tell the truth or perjure yourself. I can tell you, this doesn't look good for you."

Dave called after Murphy as he and the two men walked to his car.

"And I'm telling you the truth *now*. You say the computer is gone. I'm telling you, I have no idea who took it out of my office."

*

Jack came down the Geyser Loop trail from the golf course parking lot, with his rod and tackle box in hand.

"Daisy said you wanted to toss a line in the stream and just get away from it all," he said, nearly shouting over the sound of the fast-rushing current. Then he dropped his voice. "Who's this guy? He doesn't look like he's ready to fish for brook trout."

Andrew Samson extending a hand. "I'm Dave's criminal defense lawyer."

Dave made a half-hearted cast upstream and let his fly float back down.

"Mr. Samson here wanted to meet you somewhere where no one could overhear," he said, his voice almost lost in the rushing sound of the stream. "Not even with sophisticated listening devices."

Jack nodded at the stream. "Hence, the white noise." He looked at Dave with a concerned expression. "Well, I'm glad both of you will hear what I have to say, Andrew. It's not good news."

Dave reeled in the fly, no longer interested in keeping up the pretense.

Jack motioned them to step closer so he could lower his voice as much as possible and still be heard.

"I have a good friend who looked at Dave's personal laptop and found something very disturbing," he said quietly. "There are files in it that are encrypted."

"That's not possible; I never will." Dave started to object.

Jack held up a hand. "Let me finish. Garrett said he would be able to tell if you uploaded the files, say, from a disk or flash drive. Or if you'd downloaded them from an email. But there's no sign of that. So, they had to come from an outside source.

"After that, he looked for emails that could have delivered the files to you. He could only find one, but he couldn't find the IP address of the computer that sent it."

"What are you saying?"

"It looks like the files have come from an outside source. Someone who knew how to get access to your computer remotely. Garrett will get to the source eventually; he's that good."

Dave was furious. "So, they were planted there. What's in these files?"

"We don't know yet. He's trying to find a way to open them without them opening up as computer code gibberish. That's all he's gotten so far. I told you they're encrypted."

Andrew looked grim.

"Right. They're encrypted until they're magically opened in court, having been cracked by some so-called government computer geniuses. So that's how those bastards are trying to play this."

"Trying to be the operative," said Jack. "But they don't have the laptop now."

Andrew stopped him.

"Don't tell me where it is, because I don't want to know. Not until I need it."

"Wasn't planning to," said Jack.

*

Hannah stepped out of the café in Lake George village, laughing with Louise.

"It's been such a long time since I felt this relaxed. Thank you."

Louise had stopped laughing. "What the hell…"

She was staring at their cars, which were parked next to each other in the small lot. People had gathered on the sidewalk to watch.

Two men in suits were directing teams of three that were going through both cars. They had set contents out on the pavement: books, packages, a satchel from Louise's car that had been rifled through, bags of clothes from Hannah's intended for the thrift store.

"*What do you think?*" Hannah said, charging at them.

One of the suits held up two papers, one in each hand, and handed them to Hannah and Louise.

"We have search warrants to go through your vehicles."

"Haven't you people harassed us enough? What do you think you're going to find in my car, and why are you going through hers?"

"I'm not authorized to tell you what this search is for. And as for—" he looked at one of the papers—"as for Mrs. Thackery, her vehicle was at your home this morning."

"Just briefly, until we decided to drive here separately for lunch. For *lunch*. What is it you think she's up to?"

Louise was on her cell phone. "Les," she said in tears, "some federal agents are searching my vehicle right here in the parking lot outside the cafe." She turned and looked at the small crowd on the sidewalk. "Yes, there's a crowd watching. Why?"

"I can tell you why," said Hannah. "To embarrass and humiliate us."

"That's what Les just said."

Hannah raised her voice so all the watchers could hear.

"*This is what your government*—our *government*—*does when they want to intimidate you.*"

The federal agent holding the warrants intervened.

"Mrs. Mattson, if I were you, I'd…"

"Well, you're not me. I don't allow anyone to harass my friends without speaking up. As an American, I have the right to free speech unless you're going to tell me that's being revoked. And I'm going to tell you to your face: it's terrible enough what you're doing to us, my husband and me. But you're dragging our friends into this to put pressure on *us*. That's just low and despicable."

The agent stooped, reached into a box at his feet and lifted out a briefcase, which Louise recognized instantly.

"What are you doing with that?"

"We're confiscating it."

"Why? It's got files I need for our businesses."

"If that's all it is, then you have nothing to worry about."

Hannah was incensed. "Why take *her* briefcase?"

"She was at your home. According to your husband, other items were taken away by parties unknown. Is that truthful? I suspect it isn't. That means he's being less than cooperative and trying to play games. Maybe Mrs. Thackery is helping you now by removing papers or files needed for our investigation into your husband's illicit activities."

"*He's not involved in any illicit activities.*" Hannah almost exploded, then took deep breaths to calm herself. "When will Louise get her briefcase back?" she demanded.

"That will be up to the U.S. Attorney."

"We're all done here," said an officer from one of the search teams.

The two agents in charge turned to leave, followed by the

others.

The contents of both vehicles lay strewn around the pavement at the women's feet.

Louise threw her arms around Hannah's shoulders, which were shaking.

"I am so sorry," was all Hannah managed, before tears choked her.

"We are not backing off, Hannah. In fact, I'm glad this happened when I was with you. Now I know something about what you're going through. This is beyond wrong."

Hannah could not find her voice. The somber quiet of the Justice building in Albany weighed on Dave like a shroud. He had to take long, slow, deep breaths to keep panic from taking over.

Carl looked at him just before their footsteps sounded in the hollow corridors. "Are you okay?"

"Would you be?"

"Sorry. I mean, you look pale. Do you need a drink of water before we go in?"

"Scotch would be better."

Outside the U.S. Attorney's office suite, a very young-looking guy in a navy-blue suit stuck out his hand to Dave. "William Evers—Bill—from your malpractice insurance carrier. Here to help represent you. My office phoned you."

He looked like he should be at a college frat party, not representing anyone. Dave wanted to ask if the ink on his law school diploma was dry.

In the attorney's office, seated across from Rodriguez, Andrew Samson said, "I'll be taking the lead here on behalf of Mr. Mattson."

The young woman seated beside Rodriguez's desk angled a

small, recording device in Dave's direction and an officer standing at the door cleared his throat.

Rodriguez' face remained blank, and he ignored Samson's remark. He focused on Dave.

"Let me set things in their proper context from the beginning. I'll be conducting this interview and there will be no interruptions, no questions or comments from either one of your lawyers, Mr. Mattson."

It was stupid to think of what he was paying Samson to be here if he had to shut up and just listen, but the thought flashed through Dave's head along with all the other ways this investigation was costing him. Heavily.

Rodriguez glanced from Samson to Evers, who kept shifting in his chair. "You understand that interruptions can cause you to be removed from this room. Correct?"

"I have a question before we begin," said Evers.

Rodriguez' eyes flashed. "You have no questions. The recording has started and this is my interview."

Evers seemed to shrink in his chair.

Dave forced himself to keep his breathing steady. *Perfect. Off to a great start.*

The questioning began with a long list of queries Dave had answered a dozen times by now. In accordance with Samson's caution before the meeting, he tried to answer each one exactly as he had before—"without sounding rehearsed or like you've memorized a script."

Sure thing.

"Don't try to be clever. Don't let the guy bully or get you confused or flustered."

Not a problem.

Ten minutes in, looking at his notes, Rodriguez suddenly

became combative.

"Mr. Mattson, that's not the way you answered this question before, when Special Agent Murphy interviewed you. In fact, my notes say you gave two different answers to this same question. And now you've given me a third and different answer."

Dave felt himself tense up. "I don't recall giving a different answer before. I told Agent Murphy that I asked an assistant to handle the application because it would be good training for her, and I was busy at the time, and I would be there to answer questions for her as best I could."

"That's interesting, because you never said, 'As best I could' in your previous answer to the question, 'Who actually filled out the application?'"

"My assistant did, but I was trying to figure out exactly what was needed."

"Are you trying to imply now that you didn't know how to fill out the form and you proceeded without taking time to gain the proper information, which is criminal negligence? Or do I understand your answer to mean you had to think of a way to fill it out that would get Yusuf Abdullah the response he wanted, which is conspiracy? What exactly is your answer, Mr. Mattson, because I'm hearing you say several different things here."

"I," Dave hesitated, feeling confused and trapped, as if anything he said was going to be turned and used against him.

"Mr. Rodriguez," Andrew Samson spoke up. "My client's responses are…"

Rodriguez cut him off.

"I told you at the beginning, you are not allowed to participate in this questioning. You can sit and listen, just listen or I can have my officer remove you from this office. Is there anything about this directive that you do not understand?"

Carl had been watching Dave, and he tapped him on the arm. "You're doing fine," he said quietly. "Stay calm."

"Mr. King," Rodriguez said, his voice rising. "I just told Mr. Samson that he is not to speak, and you're talking to your client. Now you've both had a warning, and it's the only one I'll give you. Next time, you'll be escorted not only out of my office but out of the building, and you can stand in the parking lot and wait for me to finish with Mr. Mattson."

Rodriguez looked from Carl King to William Evers, who shuffled his feet and nodded.

"When I listen to this tape again later," Rodriguez concluded, glancing from one lawyer to the other, "I don't want to hear any sound of your voices on it.

"Now, Mr. Mattson, let's go back to the question I just asked you."

*

When they were outside the building, Dave quickly loosened his tie. His shirt was damp. Rodriguez' final words as they were leaving his office sounded in his head.

"I'll have to think long and hard to determine whether any of your lawyers can be present the next time you and I meet."

I can't handle it next time, Dave told himself.

"He can't bar us from an interview if you've requested that your lawyers be present," Carl fumed.

"Don't put it past Rodriguez to try to pull something like that," Samson said. "He's a thug."

William Evers rattled off something that sounded like an insurance company boilerplate statement, which Dave was too shaken to take in. He finished with something that, in Dave's mind, he could have kept to himself.

"Man, that guy is out for blood."

*

At the truck stop where Hannah insisted Dave meet her and Daisy for a mid-afternoon lunch, all the other tables were empty. The tired-looking waitress seemed totally disinterested in taking their order, let alone listening to their conversation in lowered voices.

"Where exactly is my computer now?" Dave asked, just above a whisper. "They seem to be focused on it. If you guys have it, Daisy, you need to be aware they could come looking for it."

"They already came," she said quietly, "with a search warrant and two guys to go through the house. And you're right, they really want that computer. But it wasn't at our house."

"Where..." He stopped himself. "Don't tell me. I shouldn't know."

Hannah placed a hand on Daisy's. "Just tell us you and Jack are being careful."

The waitress came with cups of coffee and seemed not to notice or care that there was no cream or sugar on the table.

Daisy was whispering now.

"Jack thinks we're under surveillance. But we're acting ridiculously normal, going to the gym, and drinking out with friends. All I'll tell you is that somewhere in the mundane mix of our lives, Jack is in touch with the forensics being done on your laptop. And before you ask, he doesn't even know exactly where it is right now. But it's in good hands."

"Just tell me, how did you get it out of our house without it being seen? Because we've been under surveillance for months."

Daisy looked at Hannah, and they smiled.

"There were piles of clothes I made her clear out of her closet," said Hannah. "I doubt that any male agents watching us paid any attention. And as for who actually carried things out of the house, well, Dave, that's none of your business."

Dave didn't know whether to feel relieved or not. His whole family was working hard to protect him. But at the same time, they were being drawn into the government's web.

Hannah's smile had vanished.

"This is what we've come to. Innocent people have to hide their actions from their own government. This feels more like Russia than the United States."

Dave forced himself to stroll slowly down the Geyser loop trail, as if he was just out for the fresh air, and also forced himself not to look around to see if anyone was following. The parking lot at the golf course appeared to be clear of government vehicles, but at this point, who knew? Obviously, the agents had tracked Hannah to the restaurant in town.

Jack was waiting for him at the spot where they had met with Andrew. The stream had risen a bit with recent rains, and the noise of the current here was even louder than before. He stepped close to Dave and kept his voice low, so low that Dave had to lean in to hear him.

"Daisy filled me in on your meeting in Albany. Damn, that sounded rough."

"Yeah, that Rodriguez, he did everything but have me measured for an orange jumpsuit and pre-assign me to a road crew."

"Don't go there."

"Too late."

"I heard your lawyers pissed him off."

"If you breathed, you pissed him off. I might have been better off not having the lawyers there."

Jack nodded. "Yeah, lawyers. Do you trust Andrew Samson?"

Dave stepped back a little. "What do you mean? Like, is he really on my side? Is he competent to handle a case like this one?"

"It would be easy enough in a case like this, with so much pressure on the defendant, to take your money upfront like they do, and then just cut a deal. Big money, very little work."

Dave stared at his boots and had to fight a sinking feeling in his gut again.

"Geez, Jack. That thought never occurred to me."

"Has he talked strategy with you?"

"Not yet. But we're just getting started."

"Bring it up soon."

"How will I even know if his defense strategy is any good? I can't afford expensive second and third opinions."

"Daisy and I just want to be sure you have no regrets later."

"Do you mean on top of the one huge regret I have already ever met or doing anything to help Yusuf Abdullah?"

"You helped him—sure, because he was being a pain in the ass and you wanted to shut him up, but also because you're a good man and you wanted to help him help starving people. Or at least that's how he sold you. Never forget you did this out of the goodness of your heart."

Dave kicked a small stone into the stream.

"Yeah, if only having a good heart could keep you out of prison."

"That's Andrew Samson's job. Let's be sure he does it."

*

Dave stared across the polished, conference room table at Andrew. He felt lightheaded.

"I know you're not kidding, but tell me you are."

"I wish I were. I know this is bad news. Very bad, actually. The U.S. Attorney called and is sending a letter to confirm. You are now officially being named as a target in the case."

"Why didn't he just say so in the meeting?"

Andrew shrugged. "He was probably hoping you'd just break right there under pressure, seeing how he could shut down your defense team and control the room."

"What does this mean?"

"It means the government intends to indict you and charge you with a felony count for filing a false application for not-for-profit status for Abdullah's Foundation, which, as we know, they're claiming is a channel for funds to terrorist and anti-American organizations."

"But they're only coming after me for the false application charge. Is that correct?"

"True, but during the government's questioning, they'll make statements about Abdullah's activities, which will throw a dark cast over your participation with him in any way. It can affect the judge's attitude toward you in terms of ruling and sentencing."

"That's just dirty."

"That's how the game is played."

Dave drummed his fingers on the table. Pressure was slowly building in his head.

"So, what do we do?"

"I may recommend that you plead guilty."

The pressure in Dave's head shot up.

"Plead guilty. That's the strategy you're proposing."

"Dave, it may be the best strategy."

"*For who?*" Jack's warning about Andrew doing as little as possible and cutting a deal sounded in the back of his mind.

"Let me just air this out for you. If you plead guilty, that puts it in the judge's hands and we can move right to sentencing. I hammer on how flimsy the government's case is against you. I can present your squeaky-clean record and even bring in character witnesses to talk about your years of service to the community and every other great thing you've ever done. We can quite possibly get you off with a slap on the wrist."

Dave started to object. "But I still *look* guilty in the eyes of the law and the public. 'Hey everyone, he even admitted it.' And that's just not."

Andrew talked over him.

"On the other hand, if you plead *not* guilty, that puts you firmly in Rodriguez' hands and he can rip you apart in court. He didn't get where he was without being a pit bull. Don't forget, there's this business about your secret computer files."

"Which don't exist."

"He made a point of bringing it up twice when we met. He's got some cards up his sleeve; he's not showing me yet."

"But doesn't the government have to present all their so-called evidence before trial, just like everyone else? And if they don't, if they try to surprise us by presenting some made-up evidence in court, you can call for a mistrial. Isn't that correct?"

"No, they can't pull that in court. But here's the gamble, Dave, and remember, though it's the legal system, with lawyers, it's all a game. The government can present all its evidence pretty much at the very last minute before a trial, giving me no time to work to counter or disprove it."

"Couldn't you ask for the trial to be delayed then, to give you time?"

"Sure. I can *ask* for anything I want. Doesn't mean the court will grant my request. The order that's come down from on high is to bring the Department of Justice and the White House scalps to wave before the public, which wants blood and convictions right now."

Dave was feeling testy. "But you *can* ask for more time if they try to pull something. I'm just trying to wrap my head around what you're willing to do for me. So, help me out here, Andrew. I feel like I'm being hung out to dry."

"What I'm willing to do is advise you from the best of my experience and knowledge. I'm telling you I know this game, and you don't want us—you and me—showing up in court with a weak case in your defense."

Dave felt like throwing a punch.

"Can't you confront Rodriguez and ask to see evidence of these so-called secret computer files now?"

"He'd laugh in my face. Or spit in it."

"Then you need to work harder on putting together a case for me."

*

The too-loud trio of young women at the next table had left the cafe, and Jen watched Dave staring at the cup of coffee he had barely sipped.

"So," he said in a moment, "are you going to keep me in suspense? Now that those loudmouths are gone, you can drop whatever bomb you're carrying."

"I thought that before we talk business, you'd at least let me buy you breakfast."

"I'm a cheap date."

"Hannah always said that about you."

He looked up from his coffee cup to see her smiling a bit and allowed himself a faint grin.

"Good to get a *little* smile out of you."

"Thanks for the offer of breakfast, but I can't eat much these days. Just tell me what you need to tell me."

"Jared Colbourn called. He heard about Hannah and her friend being stopped in public and having their vehicles searched by federal agents. He doesn't want to risk having his wife subjected to anything like that."

"He means his twenty-three-year-old girlfriend, not his wife. He hates his wife. He'd be happy if someone dragged her away."

Jen cleared her throat, and Dave could feel it coming. Colbourn Construction was one of the biggest, high-end builders in eastern New York State and a long-time client. A big account.

"And...?"

"He said to tell you he's really sorry and he thinks you're being set up. He said he's no fan of the government. You know he's kind of a lawless old redneck when he thinks he can get away with anything."

"But...?"

"He asked me to transfer all his files and records to Chatsworth and Davies. Immediately. If he owes you anything, he'll settle up."

Dave nodded. "Right. Six months from now, as usual."

"I thought I'd give you the difficult news first. There's good news, too."

"Go ahead. Make me smile."

"Three other clients, not as big as Colbourn for sure, but

good, steady people, have made it a point to call and say they are *not* pulling away from you."

As she named them, he quickly tallied up his annual charges. All three added together didn't equal half of what he billed Colbourn.

Dave took a sip of the now-cold coffee and stared into the cup. This place served crummy coffee, so why was he even drinking it?

"Before, I might have picked up the phone or driven to Colbourn's office and tried to save this piece of business."

"Before what?"

"Before I got kicked in the gut with a frozen boot, I don't have it in me to fight."

Jen sat back.

"There's one more piece of news."

"Oh lord."

"Cliff and I have discussed this and we are both in agreement."

Dave stared at her. "You're quitting. I can't blame you."

"Quitting?" She looked startled. "You know me better than that. No, Cliff and I agreed that we're willing for me to take a cut in pay if that's what it takes for you to keep me on."

A big, important client had pulled out. Three small ones were staying. And here were Jen and Cliff, willing to sacrifice to stand by him. Beyond all this, a U.S. Attorney was going to try to send him to prison as a felon. A traitor.

All at once, the instability of his situation, his future became overwhelming.

"Dave. Dave?" Jen was saying: "Are you okay?"

He tried to steady himself, calling up the faces of people who were not bailing out on him: his father, his family, some neighbors, and a couple of friends. He imagined Jen and Cliff discussing and making this heroic decision to stick with him, even if they had to sacrifice to do it.

"No," he said finally. "I'm not okay. I'm a sitting duck in the government's crosshairs. But I've got a few people around me who are fantastic human beings. The best. Including you and Cliff. That's all I can ask for right now."

Jen reached across the table and lightly squeezed his hand.

"There are more people behind you, who believe in you, than you know."

For whatever good that does me, he thought—but said, "Thank you."

*

When they walked around the corner of Jen and Cliff's house that Saturday afternoon, the sight made Dave's jaw drop.

The patio, the yard, and the perimeter of the pool—the whole space was packed with people, and every head turned. He recognized most of the people's friends, neighbors, and clients, but not everyone.

"Hey, Dave!"

"Come on, grab a beer."

"Great to see you, man."

Cliff was standing beside the grill, flipping burgers. "Take a plate. These are ready to come off the flame. Beers are in those three huge, white coolers."

Dave was still fixed in place, and Daisy and Jack stepped up beside him and Hannah. Jen appeared from the back door and joined them.

"We were getting so many calls from everyone—*these*

people," said Jen, waving a hand at the crowd, "that we decided you needed to witness all the support for you."

Dave smiled at Hannah. "You were in on this and kept it a secret. There's gotta be a hundred people here."

"We decided you needed a *good* surprise for a change."

For the next couple of hours, Dave made his way around the yard from one small group to another, shaking hands, taking in all the good wishes.

"We're with you all the way, buddy."

"You're a good guy. We believe in you."

"Best of luck, Dave."

"We're sorry about this whole situation."

When his face was sore from smiling, he settled into a corner of the yard, where five guys were talking sports, exactly what he needed to stop thinking for a while about the "situation."

Alex Hartford, his next-door neighbor, was exorcised about the Buffalo Bills as usual. "They need to do something about their starting line-up. Did you see how weak they looked in pre-season? Where's the coaching?"

"That new young receiver, he's got the hands, but the quarterback's got no arm this season. What the hell?" This, from Don Thomason, a client.

"He needs to earn that multi-million-dollar contract."

The banter rolled on for a half-hour, and Dave was tired of the sports talk when he overheard comments from the group of guys right behind him.

"They're hell-bent on convictions right now."

"This U.S. Attorney is a cold-hearted bastard. Have you ever heard him interviewed?"

"I wouldn't want to go up against him."

"I wouldn't want to go anywhere near him."

When Dave turned to join them, the conversation abruptly stopped. Of the six men staring at him, he knew three and only had a vague idea of who the others were. Guys from the neighborhood, maybe.

Les Thackery cleared his throat. "I'm sorry if you overheard any of that. We shouldn't be talking about this today."

"Don't worry about it. I know it's on everyone's mind. It's great that you all came out to help take it off mine. How's Louise, by the way? Did you ever get the briefcase back?"

Les sipped his beer, and for a moment, looked vague.

"The briefcase with your business files in it," Dave prompted. He didn't want to say, the one the agents seized, in case others in this group didn't know about the restaurant incident in which Hannah and Louise were harassed by federal agents.

"There was nothing very important in it—"

A guy who looked familiar, maybe from the neighborhood, interrupted.

"Hey, Mattson, your glass is empty. Want another beer?"

Dave shifted his attention and shook the guy's hand. "No, I'm driving."

"Come on, it's a party. Loosen up. Your wife can drive home."

Dave smirked.

"A party—in honor of me being railroaded. Jen and Cliff should have had a banner made. *Dave's Railroad Party.*"

Most of the guys smiled and the guy he didn't really know laughed.

"Railroad Party—good one."

Terry, a neighbor Dave did recognize, shook his head.

"Not really funny. Tragic, I'd say."

Chapter 12

Jack parked on the side street, walked quickly through the alley and down the five cement steps to the lower back entrance of the brownstone. The only one that wasn't run down in this seedy neighborhood of Schenectady. He rattled the bars at the door and wondered if his BMW would still be there when he came out.

"Arthur," said the very tall, stoop-shouldered guy of maybe thirty who unlocked the bars to let him in. He didn't offer a handshake, and pushed his glasses up on the bridge of his nose. "So, you found me. Most people can't."

"Well, when my buddy finally told me where my father-in-law's computer was, I did have a hard time finding you on this back street."

"That's why I bought this place."

The basement was unfinished, with painted cinder block walls, four computers, wires, six big screens, and what appeared to be telephone wires strung across the ceiling to a junction box on one outside wall. It felt sterile, with no pictures or rugs, no color—a geek's porno fantasy.

"You found something," Jack said.

Arthur sat down before one computer, which Jack recognized as Dave's and began punching keys, then moving the mouse. For a long moment, he said nothing, then he pointed at the glowing screen.

"See these files? This whole list is right here." He was grinning.

"I ran a few scans, and well, of course, nothing came up, like a point of origin IP address. They're too clever to let themselves be spotted, like any old bullshit spyware kind of program. No. Not these guys. Plus, they bank-shotted these files all around the web via a whole bunch of secret servers. So, they could have originated anywhere."

"So, you found something," Jack prompted again.

Arthur's face lit up. "*Ohhhhh* yeah. This is a set of files, and you really have to know what you're looking for and have programs that detect it. This set came in via the dark web."

"How can you tell that? Wait, don't explain. I won't get it anyway. I just need to know *what* you found."

"I only opened one and excuse me, but holy shit it's a list of terrorist sleeper cells where money should be distributed and how much each one needs."

"What about all the other files?"

"I didn't open them. *Never* open them. Never let *anyone* open them."

"Why? We need to see what's in all of them, don't we?"

"No, you don't, and here's why. If you open them, the hard drive on this laptop will register the date they were opened."

Jack hesitated, then got it.

"So, if we don't open the other files, we have two pieces of evidence: A, someone planted them via the dark web, but B, they weren't opened. Which means my father-in-law could never have had any knowledge of what's in them."

"*Ding, ding, freakin' ding.* And the only one that *was* opened, was opened today. On a date several weeks after the computer was removed from his possession."

"I'd have to testify to that," Jack said, considering. "But I took it away before the federal agents showed up with a warrant to seize it."

"… and brought it to someone for repair. Only it can't be repaired."

Jack frowned.

"Why can't it be repaired?"

"Because this old dog is pretty much useless. A piece of junk." He winked. "Which explains why it never went back to your father-in-law."

Jack stared at him, uncomprehending.

"When they ask, you can tell them your tech said, 'It was a train wreck, not worth fixing.' And it went to the landfill."

Jack smiled and nodded.

"*But* I can leave enough of its little brain intact so that any good forensic technician, who has to testify, can find and explain what I just showed you that just *one file* in this whole life was opened on *this* date.

"By the way, if you need to call a tech into court to testify to that, it won't be me. I keep my head way down. But I can recommend someone good. Better than good."

Jack nodded. "You really can do that—set this computer up exactly the way you just said?"

Arthur smiled. "You insult me. I can have it done in a couple of hours and then you can have your zombie laptop back."

Out in his car, Jack put the key in the ignition and a wave of anger slammed him along with clarity about the scheme.

Present the computer as evidence in court. Show the list of files from anti-American organizations, and open them one by one. No one else in the courtroom has any knowledge that the files were never opened before that moment… And Dave is nailed to the cross.

He slammed his hands on the steering wheel.

What sonofabitch would go to this length to set up an innocent man?

*

The halls of the Justice Center sounded hollower and felt colder than Dave remembered, as if they could engulf and swallow a man whole. He was sure they had, many times.

In Rodriguez's office, the atmosphere was even more somber, in a way that reminded Dave of a funeral parlor.

"Mr. Mattson," Rodriguez went right for it. "You're here because I want to give you a chance to enter a plea before we take this case to court."

Dave looked at Andrew Samson. "Were you aware this was the purpose of this meeting today?"

Samson started to reply, but Rodriguez cut him off.

"The same rules apply in this meeting as last time. You address only me, Mr. Mattson, and your attorney is just here to observe, not to comment on or advise you. At least it was a smart move on your part not to bring your whole legal entourage this time."

He leaned forward.

"How do you plan to plead?"

"I'm not guilty. I didn't do anything wrong. I made a simple mistake."

Rodriguez pivoted his chair a little, to look out the window. He had on his face what Dave assumed passed for a smile.

"I'm not sure why you want to waste the government's and the court's time, Mr. Mattson. As I look over the evidence, this is an open and shut case. Period."

"I'm not guilty."

"More evidence will come out. You know the investigation is ongoing."

"I'm not guilty."

"Do you think we'd waste our time going forward to trial, which we will if the government wasn't convinced of your wrongdoing? Do you think you're being persecuted?"

He paused, to let his next question land like a mortar shell.

"Is that why you referred to your assistant's afternoon soirée as a 'Railroad Party'?"

It was well-aimed. An explosion went off in Dave's brain, and the faces of six men flashed before his mind's eye. Which one had posed as a friendly supporter, but was there to spy on him and report everything he said? Who was hoping he'd slip up and admit to something that could help hang him?

Andrew Samson was shifting in his chair, as if he was fighting hard against the urge to speak.

Dave recovered enough to reply.

"If the purpose of this meeting is to know how I'm going to plead, you have my answer.

I plead *not guilty*."

*

Outside on the sidewalk, Dave was still shaking. What had just happened was unsettling and he was pissed at Andrew.

"I didn't know for sure what the meeting was about, Dave," Andrew said pre-emptively before Dave could speak.

"But Rodriguez pressing to know how I'll plead was a definite possibility, right? You could have mentioned that."

Andrew shifted the focus off himself. "Your best option, quite frankly, is to plead guilty."

The thought crossed Dave's mind that he'd never heard a lawyer apologize or admit they'd screwed up, but that was beside the point right now.

"Whose side are you on?" he nearly shouted.

"Yours."

"It sure as hell doesn't seem like it."

Andrew squared his shoulders. "Calm down and listen to me. He may not be bluffing when he says that they have, or soon will have more evidence against you to present in court. That's a big risk for us to take and I can't ignore that.

"Second, if you plead guilty, you avoid a big, overblown, media circus trial. I'm playing the long game here. If you plead guilty, you avoid all that exposure for you and your family. And when the dust settles, you can always accept a few, select media interviews where you explain what you were pleading guilty to: negligence versus anti-American activities."

Dave was feeling sick.

"That *sounds* like a great plan, but it'll be too late. People always think there must have been something to the charges. Where there's smoke. They'll think, 'Oh, he just had a lawyer who played some legal tricks got him off.' In the eyes of the public, I'll still be guilty of *something*, and they'll fill in the blanks themselves as to what that terrible thing really is."

Andrew stood his ground.

"I know you can't see it at this moment, but trust me. It's absolutely your best option. Unless you really want to give the government a chance to dump buckets of red paint all over you and convince the judge at sentencing that you deserve to spend a lot of time in a federal prison."

*

Dave's hands shook as he drove home and he wondered if he should be driving at all. He kept going over the list of American citizens or lawful residents of the U.S. that Andrew had just reminded him about all the men the government had gone after and won convictions for.

Three were African-Americans, two were from families that originated in Pakistan, one was born in Virginia to Palestinian immigrants, one was from New York and was the son of Afghani parents, and two were young white men from Texas who had converted to Islam. The list went on and on.

All were convicted and sent to prison.

He had calmed his shaking, but not his thoughts.

In his head, a television news story replayed the one about Elias Koutab, a hardworking young father of three who'd emigrated to America to give his family a better life. He saw the angry face of Koutab's lawyer and heard again his impassioned words almost verbatim.

"... A gross injustice has been done to my client, because the prosecutor has claimed that the documents filed with the judge are protected under recent anti-terrorist... and we can't have access to them.

"How are we to prepare... if the government claims it has the right to conceal information from thousands of pages of alleged documentation it supposedly has in its possession? We don't even know all the charges against him, so we're being kept in the dark. Unless I can shake the heavens and get access to the evidence and the charges, Mr. Koutab will go on trial without a well-prepared defense."

Dave's throat was dry.

The government could literally do anything it wanted to him, and his lawyer was advising him to just roll over and plead guilty.

*

"Dave, where are you?"

He could hear Hannah walking through the house from room to room, searching for him. Obviously, she'd seen his car in the driveway.

He turned his face to the wall and buried his head deeper under a pillow.

The light switch clicked on.

"What are you doing in here in the den in the dark? Why didn't you answer my phone calls? I've been worried sick."

He clenched his eyes tighter.

Not as sick as you're going to be.

A hand settled gently on his shoulder.

"Please sit up and tell me what's happening."

Seated upright on the sofa, with Hannah beside him, he felt as if everything—the room, the house, the world—was surreal.

"They're going to convict me. I'll go to prison."

"We'll have friends attest to your character. Maybe the judge will be lenient."

She sounded like a woman desperately grasping at straws.

"Our friends are traitors. We can't trust any of them."

"Stop. You saw all the support for you at your party. You're sounding paranoid now."

He told her about Rodriguez' knowledge of his "Railroad Party" statement.

She took a deep breath, but said nothing.

"It could have been Les Thackery. When I asked him if they'd recovered Louise's briefcase with the important papers, he acted at first like he didn't even know about it. Then he recovered and said what was in it was no big deal. But you told me how upset Louise was and how she'd insisted it had important files in it."

"Dave, I don't know. Maybe she was just upset and saying anything to keep her case from being seized."

"When we were on the golf course, Les was asking me a lot of questions."

"Stop."

"What did you tell Louise? You've got to remember every word you said."

"*Stop*. These people are among our best friends."

"What if the government says the IRS has something on them and they've been offered immunity from prosecution if they deliver evidence to be used against me?"

Hannah stood up quickly.

"Don't. I just can't." She was wringing her hands. "I can't handle it if our friends are really turning against us. I can't; I won't believe that." She charged out of the den in tears.

Dave sat for a long time before getting up to switch off the light again. Faintly, he could hear Hannah sobbing somewhere in another room. Then he returned to the sofa, laid down, and buried his head under the pillow again.

Weeks ago, he'd thought he was at the bottom and couldn't sink any lower. Now, over and over, one carrion thought circled.

I'm a dead man… I'm a dead man…

*

Jen's face was set in an angry expression.

"Agent Murphy is here again."

Dave had been sitting at his desk, staring out the office window, for how long, he wasn't even sure. Maybe all morning. He didn't reply, and just nodded.

When Murphy stepped into the room, with two men following him, Dave didn't look at them and continued staring out the window.

"I have another warrant here."

"I guess you guys forgot to search the tank on the back of the toilet."

Murphy made a disgusted sound.

"Sarcasm won't help your case."

Like anything will help my case at this point.

"To save us both time, we're looking for your home computer. If it's here, you can hand it over now, or we will have to take the place apart looking for it. Your call."

Vaguely, Dave thought, *Why the big interest in my laptop?*

"I can tell you it's not here. But I'm sure that won't stop you from looking. Be my guest."

In an hour, the search over, Murphy was back standing in front of Dave's desk.

Good God, if looks could kill.

"It could help your case if you cooperate and turn it over."

Dave almost laughed, but resisted the urge.

"It was taken from my home."

Murphy's face had turned red. "Who took it?"

"I don't know."

Murphy sounded angry now. "I believe you do."

He's losing it. Isn't that just too bad?

"I'll swear to it under oath. I don't know."

"We *will* find it."

Dave knew he shouldn't goad Murphy, but couldn't stop

himself.

"The thing is old. Half the time, I can't find things I've saved. It's probably not worth your trouble."

Murphy looked as if a bowstring had snapped inside him. Whatever was left of his cool, in-charge demeanor vanished in a second.

"If anything's been tampered with or any files have been deleted," he snapped, "it's going to go very badly for you."

When Murphy was gone, Jen stepped back in.

"Why the hell is he so interested in your computer?"

Dave felt exhausted.

"My guess is that he was supposed to seize it when they raided my home office. But you should have seen him; he was almost giddy when he found a piece of paper in a file that had phone numbers of mosques and Islamic centers on it. He acted like he'd found the holy grail, but I'll bet that made him forget he was supposed to seize the laptop, too. When he didn't show up with it, Rodriguez probably tore him a new one."

Jen smiled through her grim expression.

"If so, I really hope it hurts."

*

Dave woke in the half-light the next morning, coming out of a dream in which he kept listing over and over the people who were on his side. He'd name a few, then get confused were they or weren't they, really, and have to start over.

Hannah was gently shaking his shoulder.

"You keep saying, 'Hannah, Daisy, Jack...'" over and over. Why don't you come downstairs? Coffee's ready and I'm making waffles."

Sunlight streaming in through the rear kitchen windows felt too bright and piercing.

"Can we drop these shades?"

"And sit here in gloom? No."

Hannah set a steaming cup in front of him and turned to the waffle iron with its blinking light. "This one's done."

"I might skip breakfast, if you don't mind."

"As it happens, I do mind. You've got to come around, Dave. I know how heavy all this is weighing on you. I know," she wouldn't say the name, "that agent's visit yesterday did more damage to your psyche. You know that's what it was supposed to do, right?"

"It worked."

"We've got to keep our fighting spirit. You have to keep a fighting spirit. You've got to keep up your strength, and face to the sun." She smiled at him. "And you need waffles. They always make you happy."

He made himself smile.

"That looks more like a grimace."

That got a chuckle out of him.

"*Better*," she said, smiling and setting the plate in front of him. "Now eat. I didn't make your favorite breakfast to have you turn it down. And when you're done, put dirty dishes in the dishwasher, please, not on the counter."

"Where's yours?"

"I've got an early meeting at work and need to run."

In another moment, she was out the door.

Dave took a bite of a waffle and reached for the coffee cup. She was right. He had to believe things could still turn out okay. Somehow.

A scream came from out in the driveway, and he leapt up,

knocking on the table and spilling his coffee.

Out on the front walk, Hannah stood frozen with her hands up to her face. "Ohmygod, ohmygod, *ohmygod,* who would do this?" She pointed to Dave's car and began to sob.

On the trunk, someone had spray-painted in bright red the word:

TRAITOR

When the police arrived, Hannah was still shaking with anger.

"No, we don't have security cameras."

"Might be a good idea," said one of the officers, "under the circumstances, don't you think?"

Was that an edge of irony or sarcasm? Dave couldn't tell.

"There are cameras at different places in the neighborhood. Maybe they captured something useful," he suggested.

"Maybe and maybe not."

Hannah stared at him. "But you'll check, right?"

"Most likely."

Most likely?

The second officer was standing with arms folded across his chest.

Dave turned to him. "Do you think there's any chance whoever did this might have touched the trunk and left fingerprints?"

"Unlikely, I'd say. And if you look closely, there's a fine film of dust on your car. Fingerprints don't show up very well when there's that much dust."

"I ran my car through the car wash two days ago."

The officer pressed his lips together and said nothing.

The first officer closed his little notepad.

"We've got your information. Someone will get back to you

if we find out anything."

"Wait a minute," Hannah stepped in. "My husband's car has been vandalized, and you don't seem at all interested. You haven't been here for twenty minutes or even examined the car."

He shot a sideways glance at his partner, who seemed to be fighting to keep a smirk off his face. "We have a lot of calls to follow up on. A lot of good citizens in this town need our attention this morning. Like I said, someone, we'll get back to you if we find out anything."

Inside, Hannah stormed around the kitchen.

"They aren't the least bit interested in helping us. Did you hear how he slipped the knife in *'good citizens'* need their attention?"

Silently, Dave wiped up the spilled coffee.

He thought, but didn't say, *if we thought we could count on police support or protection, we were dead wrong.*

Chapter 13

Jack stood at the backdoor of Arthur's brownstone, rattling the bars.

"Hey man, it's me. I've been calling you for days."

Given Arthur's apparent paranoia and making it clear he kept his work secret, he didn't add, "I came for the laptop."

He'd driven all this way, though, and wasn't leaving. He rattled the bars again.

The back door opened a crack, and Arthur's face appeared. Then it opened wider.

"Come inside. Quick. Did anyone follow you? Anyone watching?"

Jack almost said, "I don't think so," but went with, "No. Why? What's going on?"

"Someone hacked into my computers."

"All of them?"

"I said *computers*, didn't I? Every one of them is riddled with viruses. Every one of them could still melt down. I keep waiting for shoes to drop."

Jack nodded and said nothing as Arthur stooped and picked up a box. Inside, it was Dave's computer.

"This thing's a 'zombie' now, right? Like you said it would be."

Arthur sounded angry and impatient. "Like I said it would be."

"Do you know who hacked you?"

Arthur shoved the box hard into Jack's arms. "Do I know? Of *course*, I know."

"The Government?"

Arthur stared at him like he was an idiot.

"Do you think they did anything with the files you took off Dave's computer? I mean, did they retrieve them? Can they prove those files were on his computer?"

Arthur looked like he wanted to cry or hit Jack. He pushed a business card at him.

"This is the guy you want to summon as a witness in court. This guy, *not* me. He's actually someone they called in a couple of times as an expert witness, so he knows all the tricks."

Jack had stepped out the back door with the box in his arms. He turned to Arthur, "How do I know for sure this guy will want to help us and?"

"You don't," said Arthur, and shut the door hard.

"You're telling me you don't have the computer? Just flat out, don't have it."

Agent Murphy squared his shoulders, ready for what would come next.

"No, sir."

Rodriguez nodded, and his voice remained calm. "You aren't leaving a trail, are you?"

Murphy hated when Rodriguez was this placid sounding. It could be like the stillness before a volcano blew or heads rolled.

"We knew who was working on trying to trace us, but we shut him down."

"But *no computer*."

"That's correct, sir."

Standing, Rodriguez walked back and forth across the office carpet twice, then again.

"Agent Murphy, *you* told me," Rodriguez began...

No, you told me. Murphy objected silently, *that you strongly believed there were files on Mattson's computer that would nail him. But you sure as hell didn't say how you knew that.*

"... That you neglected to seize Mattson's computer when you had the chance. And you told me that if I gave you access to my resources, you could get into that computer the next time it was online. And now you're telling me, you've failed to do that."

Murphy could see how this was stacking up. *You offered me the resources without my asking.*

Rodriguez stood in front of the wall where he had posted more articles about people arrested and being held on suspicion of terrorist, anti-American conspiracies.

"I'm sure... very sure I've made it clear about the orders that came down."

"You have, sir, yes."

"Let me tell you about a new directive. Midterm elections are coming up. The party in power is dropping in the polls because we're not winning the war in Afghanistan, and no weapons of mass destruction were ever found in Iraq during that war. The left is getting louder. They want every bit of ammunition they can get in their hands to hold onto power."

Murphy nodded. "I'll stay on it."

Rodriguez repeated, his tone just shy of mocking. "You'll stay on it. That's one hundred percent correct. Because more convictions are needed to wave at the public."

Walking down the corridor, Agent Murphy felt the urge to kick something.

And if you don't land this conviction, Mr. Rodriguez, I know who's set up to take the fall.

"Isn't that your Agent Murphy?" said Andrew Samson, nodding at the figure crossing the street to the parking garage.

"That's him. Just a prince of a guy," Dave replied. "Probably here to plan my execution."

"No gallows humor," Andrew reprimanded.

In Rodriguez' office, the atmosphere was as much like a mausoleum as Dave thought of it on his previous visits. The woman who had been there the previous time aimed a recording device in Dave's direction.

"I want to know what you know about Yusuf Abdullah's wife's activities in his non-profit organization."

Dave shrugged. "I know nothing about that. Zero."

Rodriguez tapped the tips of his fingers together. "I'm going to ask you again, and give you a chance to make a truthful answer. What do you know about Mrs. Abdullah's involvement?"

"I told you the honest truth the first time. I do not know anything about her involvement or if she even had any."

"The 'honest truth.' Interesting way to phrase that."

Andrew's leg bumped Dave's lightly and Dave got the message. *"He's goading you."*

"That's correct. I never met with her in regard to Dr. Abdullah's organization. Not once."

"You never met with her in regard to the organization. Did you ever meet her on any occasion for any matter?"

"I met her at one or two social functions in the community."

"So, you did meet with her."

Dave was feeling uncomfortable already, just the way, he supposed, Rodriguez wanted him to feel.

"I said I *met* her. You know, to shake hands and chat informally. I didn't meet *with* her."

"What were these informal chats about?"

"I don't recall."

Rodriguez frowned.

"Doctor Abdullah was an important client, and you met his wife and 'chatted,' you say. But you don't recall what about."

"That's correct. Maybe we talked about."

Andrew's knee bumped Dave's again and he stopped mid-sentence.

Rodriguez' face went red.

"Mr. Samson, you were strictly warned during our very first conference not to interfere in any way in these meetings. And if you think I can't see you signaling your client to stop talking, you're mistaken. Now you need to leave my office."

Andrew stood and leaned close to the recorder.

Dave almost shouted, *"Don't say anything to piss him off."*

"I'm going on record as witnessing that you twisted my client's words."

Rodriguez' hands were clenched.

"Go. Now. Before I have you detained."

Andrew opened his mouth as if to say something, but seeing Dave's pleading look that said *"Don't do it,"* he rose and exited the room.

Facing Rodriguez alone, Dave felt like a small animal in a cage with a predator.

"My best recollection, and it's vague because it was small talk, is that Mrs. Abdullah and I traded simple pleasantries and I think discussed good restaurants in the area."

"That's all? Nothing about bank transfers?"

"Nothing like that at all," Dave said. He felt like this was going out on a limb. "May I inquire why you're asking about that?"

Rodriguez ignored him.

"Mr. Mattson, we have enough evidence to charge Dr. Abdullah with multiple crimes against the United States of America. And you know how it is when a large sailing vessel goes down." He paused and waited.

"I don't mean to be difficult," Dave responded, "but I'm not sure what you're getting at."

"When a large vessel does down, it pulls all the smaller vessels around it right down with it."

Dave said nothing. Clearly, this meeting was as much about intimidation as gathering information.

"Sir, I know nothing about Mrs. Abdullah's involvements. I don't even know if she's in a gardening club."

Rodriguez smiled—a look with no warmth.

"Here's what you need to know. We have enough evidence to convict Dr. Abdullah of so many crimes that we're going to bury him. And bury him so deep he'll never see sunlight again."

There was a long silence in which Dave could feel his heart pounding in his neck.

"Anyone who helped him would do well to give up evidence that helps us instead."

*

Andrew was waiting in the hall outside the office suite.

"You all right?"

Dave turned to him. "Why the hell did you do that? You pissed him off royally."

"I knew he was going to toss me and I wanted to go on record as challenging him. I wanted it to be there in the official transcript of this interview, which I'm going to subpoena."

Something else had been in the back of Dave's mind.

"How did you know that was Murphy crossing the street before?"

"What do you mean?"

"He wasn't in our previous meetings. How do you know what he looks like?"

Andrew opened his mouth and started talking and to Dave, it sounded like he wasn't sure where his answer was going. "I... did some homework... I like to know my adversaries... So, I hunted him up online."

"Seriously? You're telling me you can find information and pictures of federal agents online?"

Andrew nodded. "Yes. Sure. If you know someone who's a computer wizard."

Dave was silent.

"Look," said Andrew, "we've still got a month before your case goes to trial. We should talk about how you're going to plead."

Dave fought to keep from exploding.

"Not. Guilty."

Andrew placed a hand on his shoulder.

"We'll talk about it."

All the way home, Dave realized that, with time running out fast before his trial, he was less and less comfortable with Andrew Samson.

*

"What are you saying?" Hannah prompted. "You want to fire

your lawyer? Isn't it a bit too late for that? We can't start over with someone new this far into the game."

Dave paced the front room, running his hands through his hair.

"He recognized Murphy when he'd never met him in person. He said he knows someone who's a wiz with computers."

"So... you think Andrew Samson has secretly switched sides and is really working for the government?"

"Could be."

"And you think some of our best friends are spying on us."

"Don't make it sound like I'm crazy, Hannah."

"You sound crazy."

Dave swiped a small porcelain dish off an end table and it smashed into the brick hearth. Then he rubbed both hands over his face.

"*David.* You've got to calm down."

He swore. "I'm sorry. I'll replace the dish."

"I don't care about the damn dish. I don't want to rush you to the emergency room again."

"I just don't know how much more pressure I can take."

"They're *trying* to break you. It makes sense to me, given all the stress you're under, that you'd start distrusting everyone, even people who are here to help and support you. Don't let them get away with it."

"I feel like I could blow my brains out."

Hannah stepped up and slapped him hard across the face.

"Don't you ever, *ever* say that again. How dare you, when you have so many who love you and will stick by you no matter what."

He took long, slow, deep breaths.

"You're right. I'm sorry. I'll get ahold of myself."

He wrapped his arms around Hannah, and she leaned into him and held on.

"I love you," he said quietly.

"I have always loved you," she said, pressing her cheek against his chest. "And I'll never stop loving you."

He squeezed her tight.

Even when they bury me in prison?

Chapter 14

The nursing home attendant seemed reluctant to answer, as he pointed Dave to the sunroom.

"I said, how's Evelyn today?" Dave repeated.

The attendant cleared his throat. "We're not supposed to comment on a resident's condition, but," he lowered his voice, "I think she's not doing very well. The docs have increased her heart meds and she's skipping meals."

When he found her in her usual chair, though she was impeccably dressed as usual and her hair was still done up perfectly, she looked more frail.

"Seated on your throne, holding court, I see."

"Over the blind, the lame, and the halt."

Dave looked around at the two other residents sitting nearby and held a finger up to his lips.

She waved a hand at him. "Neither one of them can hear. A freight train could come through."

"Hannah said you called and wanted to see me. Are you okay? I understand you're not eating like you should."

"That damn Michael. He told you that, didn't he? Snitch."

"Easy. He's just watching out for you."

"We're here to talk about you, not me. I understand that you're not doing very well."

"So, you can have your snitch, but I can't have mine."

She slapped the arms of her chair with both hands.

"Yes, I've been keeping tabs on you. Hannah tells me

everything. Now listen to me. *You must not let the government get to you.* If you do, they will have won before you even walk into that courtroom."

He let out a long breath.

"I'm trying."

"Try harder. Let me tell you something I haven't told anyone before."

She hesitated and she looked away, as if letting her mind go back in time.

"My father, rest his soul; he gave up on life after the government came after him. Oh, he was still *there* physically, but he was a shell of a man. He let the prosecutor and all the friends who turned away from him grind down his soul." She fell silent, as if she should say more, but didn't. "You can't let that happen to you."

"I don't know if I can stop it from happening to me."

She snapped back to the present.

"It's happening right now. I can tell."

"You can? How?"

"You came slouching in here and you're slouching at this very moment. Come over here."

He stood in front of her armchair.

"Straighten up."

He stiffened his back.

"Now put out your hand. Palm up."

He obeyed.

She reached out one hand, doubled into a fist, and held it above his open palm.

"Here," she said firmly, opening her hand.

Dave stared at his palm.

"What did you just do?"

"I just gave you a backbone and a new pair of balls to hang on it."

"Ouch."

"They ruined my father. I will not let them ruin you. I saw your face when you came in."

"They're already winning."

"Sometimes you win by playing the long game. Take the hit, and be a man."

"Have you been talking to my lawyer?"

"I've been reading up on these matters, David. If you plead guilty, you can avoid a trial. Judges have the discretion to waive serious penalties and go light. If your lawyer leans heavily on a 'simple negligence' defense."

"That's *if* he claims 'simple negligence.' I'm not sure about him."

"Oh, you can be sure about him. Hannah gave me his name. I already spoke to him. I told him exactly what he needs to do, and I told him he's not going to bill you or me for the paltry fifteen minutes we talked on the phone."

Dave stared at her.

"You're a warrior."

"So are you. Now go *fight*."

He smiled, then started to laugh. "You're killin' me, Evelyn."

"Now I'm going to kill that snitch, Michael. On your way out, send him in here."

"Oh, no. Let's make a deal. You leave my snitch alone and I'll leave yours alone."

Sitting at his desk, he called out to Jen.

"No calls for a while, okay?"

"Got it," she called back.

He stared out the window.

"Now go fight."

It was a great pep-talk. And it had almost worked. His mind was a mass of confusion.

Should he trust Andrew Samson, or fire him and get a new defense lawyer... or was it already too late in the game for that? The judge, under pressure from the government, might force the trial to go on anyway, whether Dave's side was well prepared or not.

And how should he plead?

Guilty? But I'm not guilty.

If he pled guilty and threw himself at the mercy of the court, he would most certainly lose everything—his friends, his business. And if the court was not merciful, so was his freedom.

He was wrong before when he thought he was at the bottom. This was a sub-basement. He saw his future—everything—rushing down a dark drain.

Leaning forward, he crossed his arms on the desk and sank his face into them, wishing for oblivion.

Chapter 15

Andrew Samson looked unsettled.

"What is he doing here?" he said, nodding toward Carl King, who was sitting across the conference room table.

"We're getting ready to go to trial soon," Dave replied, "and I want him to weigh in on strategy. I trust him."

The last sentence didn't appear to land well on Samson.

"You get two lawyers in a room; you wind up with ten opinions and they all conflict," Andrew responded quickly.

Dave was remembering his visit with Evelyn.

"No. Today, we wind up with one opinion. *Mine.* I'm the one whose life is going to be affected by the strategy we determine. You guys have been paid already, whether or not I get an orange jumpsuit."

Carl and Andrew both started to speak and Dave held up a hand.

"Here's what's going to happen. Listen."

He straightened up in his chair. "I'm going to plead not guilty, and you, Andrew, are going to refute all the so-called evidence they present against me. I'm going to walk out of that courtroom with my name cleared."

Andrew stared at him for a long moment of silence before replying. Then he leaned forward, elbows on the table, looking him directly in the eye.

"You really don't seem to get this. I was sure you did. But you don't."

"Yeah, I sure as hell do. Nothing is more important to me than clearing my name."

"Dave, these people aren't playing fair and square. You *know* this. They can make any charge against you they want and not present any evidence to back it up, claiming it's a matter of national security that they keep it a secret. It's the same bullshit they pull in Israel when the government there wants to prosecute Palestinians. It's called 'secret charges.' They don't even have to say what those charges are. It's the equivalent of the government saying, 'Just trust us, this guy's guilty.'"

"Now our government is using that strategy here, and our judges are being pressured to go along with this and turn in scalps."

"I want my name cleared," Dave said, his voice getting louder.

Andrew slammed his hands on the table.

"Do you want your name cleared? Or do you want your freedom?"

The starkness of the either-or proposition hung in the air.

"If I say I'm guilty, then what?"

"Then I can pursue the 'simple negligence' defense your friend Evelyn knew about."

"Why can't you do that if I plead not guilty."

"I can, but here's the thing: If you plead guilty, it will spare you, the court and the judge a lengthy trial, and the judge may like that and look much more favorably on giving you a lighter sentence."

"'May' is the operative word, though, isn't it? He or she also may not be affected by whatever I plead and side with the government for brownies and career points."

Dave stood up fast, almost knocking over his chair.

"I am not going to plead guilty."

Carl was shaking his head.

"You've got to think about it, Dave."

Andrew kept his voice level.

"Why did you hire me, if you're not going to trust my opinion and experience?"

"I hired you because he said I should," Dave answered, nodding at Carl.

"So, you're not going to rely on both your lawyers giving you their best advice."

"Not at the moment—no."

Andrew drummed his fingers on the table.

"So, we're headed to trial shortly, and we don't have a strategy."

*

"That's how your meeting ended?" said Hannah. "In a stalemate with your lawyers? Dear God."

They had driven to a local park, for air and quiet. As they walked the rolling pathways, it was clear that peace wasn't on the cards.

"It ended with Andrew Samson telling me I should consider hiring another lawyer or make up my mind to trust him."

Hannah stopped walking.

"Is there a reason you don't trust Andrew? Because that's what I've started to pick up."

"I didn't tell you this, but—"

"Dammit, David, this has to stop—you are not telling me things. I'm not a little girl you have to protect."

He attempted to lighten the mood a little.

"I don't know, Hannah." He smiled weakly. "Everything I tell you goes right to Evelyn."

"This is not time for kidding around. Talk."

"I was about to. Here's the thing. Andrew recognized Agent Murphy when we saw him at a distance crossing a street at the Justice Center. They'd never met before, and when I asked Andrew how he knew what Murphy looked like, he gave me an answer I couldn't buy. 'Some computer whiz I know looked up his picture online. I wanted to see what the enemy looked like.'"

Hannah was looking off into the air.

"Do you know my friend Casandra, who's head librarian in the main library in Albany?"

"Why?"

"Because she has an advanced degree in library sciences. I happen to know from talking to her that she has access to advanced search engines that give her ten times the information you and I could ever come up with by ourselves online."

"That came up in casual conversation?"

"She told me she had just helped her husband get his Ph.D. in ancient, pre-biblical languages. She knew how to get him access online to a very rare dictionary that exists only in the old church in the Middle East, one that translates Ugaritic, which is the mother tongue of both Hebrew and Arabic, into English."

Dave stared.

"And?"

"If she has access to that kind of impossible-to-find information, I can believe that Andrew Samson was able to find a picture of Agent Murphy somewhere online. Who knows, maybe his computer whiz hacked into a government computer and he didn't tell you that."

Dave started walking again, saying nothing, and Hannah had

to catch up.

"What do you want me to do, Hannah?"

"I want you to trust him and consider the strategy he suggests."

"Plead guilty; let him argue that what I did was 'simple negligence,' not the act of a home-grown terrorist, then what? Cross our fingers and hope the judge isn't in a hanging mood?"

"When I consider what Andrew explained—that the government can say anything they want against you and they don't even have to present evidence—*yes*. That's what I'm suggesting."

He picked up the pace a little, taking the bend in the path that led back to the parking lot.

When they reached the car, he looked across the roof of it at her.

"No."

"No? Just *no?*"

"Just no."

They rode in silence until they reached home. In the driveway, before getting out, she looked across at him.

"I love you, David. But you can be a stubborn, pig-headed man."

"My *name* is at stake, Hannah."

"So is my *future*, and that could be me living without you for years and growing old alone."

Andrew had the relaxed attitude of a guy getting ready to go on vacation—no suit jacket, open collar, no tie—but if that was supposed to make Dave feel relaxed, it failed. He was irritated.

"Let's talk about the plea," Andrew began.

"We've discussed this. Not guilty."

Andrew nodded, and his brow furrowed.

"Then there's a big chance we'll be blindsided by whatever the Government claims they have in evidence against you but will say they can't present because of national security reasons. It's an unfair card from another deck only they have, but they can and will play it."

"I'd rather go to prison with my head held high and my name and honor intact."

Carl King was tapping his foot under the table.

"What about taking the chance that you won't go to prison at all? Dave, if you plead guilty and Andrew argues for simple negligence, we will hold a press conference immediately after the trial and explain your plea and what it really meant."

"People will only hear 'he pled guilty' and figure that the claim of 'simple negligence' was just a white-collar criminal wiggling his way out of punishment for his crime."

Andrew's relaxed attitude was gone.

"Let me be honest. I will fight like hell for you, Dave. But read the room. The government is slam-dunking people all over the place. I hate to put it this starkly, but—"

Carl stopped tapping his foot and looked like someone had just died or was about to.

"There's a strong chance," Andrew continued, "that we're going to lose if we go to trial, and you'll go to prison. For a long time. By the time you get out, you'll be an old man. So, you've got to think, is that what you want? Fighting for a verdict of 'simple negligence' is your best shot."

Dave was done.

"All right, so I plead guilty, but we all know I'm not."

Andrew let out a long breath.

"That doesn't work."

"What the hell are you talking about?"

Carl stepped in.

"Samson here seemed to think I'd have a different opinion, but I don't. Your lawyer can only enter a guilty plea if you tell us you're guilty."

Dave felt a sudden pressure in his chest. In his mind's eye, he saw himself in the emergency room or in a cell. And Hannah's words came back.

"My future could be me living without you for years and growing old alone."

The floor seemed to fall out from under him and the walls closed in.

"Basically, my choice of how to plead lies somewhere between terrible and horrible and self-inflicted."

*

Dave stared at his office computer screen, looking through the client's IRS forms for the third time, then looked at the company's bookkeeping files for the fourth time.

Outside, it was a brilliant, sunny day, and he dropped his hands and stared out the window.

Jen came in with two cups of coffee, set one on his desk and kept one.

"Do you want to talk?"

"About what?"

"About the fact that the grand jury is meeting today to decide whether or not the government has enough credible evidence to move your case on to trial."

He scoffed.

"There's no 'whether or not.' There is no need for 'credible evidence.' The government has already made up its mind, and

God only knows how they're pulling big strings and influencing grand juries and judges to do their bidding."

"Dave, you're *not guilty*. You have to hold onto that."

He rubbed his temples. She had no idea the position he was in and he had no energy to explain it. She also had no idea that her vote of confidence was flying in the face of his lawyers' advice and wasn't helping right now.

"I may not be guilty, but I should not have half-assed that application for Abdullah. The government and the courts will not accept, 'I was distracted by tax season and my daughter's wedding, and even though my name was going on the form, I irresponsibly gave the work to an inexperienced, new assistant.' One way or another, Jen, I'm going down. I can feel it. I *know* it."

Jen stared at her coffee, then back at him.

"No matter what, Dave, we're with you."

I'll be sure to put your name on the prison's list of approved visitors.

Hannah turned off the five o'clock news as soon as Dave turned it on.

"Didn't Andrew or Carl call to tell you the decision?"

"They did. Of course."

"Then why do you want to hear it broadcast all over the place? Why do that to yourself? I sure as hell don't want to hear it."

"I guess I want to hear what everyone else is hearing. I want to know what's in everyone's head when I run into them or when I call a client."

"You need to stop that 'what everyone else is *thinking*' business. It only matters what we *know*."

"Two more clients pulled out today. One big one. So…"

She opened her mouth to speak, then didn't.

The phone rang.

"Evelyn just called me with the news," said the voice at the other end, his father's.

"It's being broadcast far and wide, Dad. Dave Mattson, indicted on charges of fraud and possible conspiracy."

"Bastards."

"Be careful, Dad; my phone line may be bugged."

"In that case, *lousy bastards*."

He heard Hannah pick up on the extension.

"Hello, Pop. I need to hear your voice, too. This is that 'rock and hard place' you hear about."

"You're strong people. You can do this. But do you need me to come up there?"

"No," Dave replied. "And I wish Evelyn would stay out of this. She has enough to think about with her health."

"Given what happened to her father? There's no way. He was such a great friend, and totally innocent. She's ready to fight. So am I."

Dave's spirit lightened a little.

"We believe in you, Hannah, me, Daisy, your true friends. You're a good man, son. We know you're innocent. Don't cave in."

Clashing advice rang inside his head. And for the second time in a couple of hours, he thought, *I appreciate it, but this isn't helping.*

*

He found Hannah seated on the edge of the bed, the phone receiver still in her hand, though the call was over.

"I love your father; you know I do."

"But."

"No one seems to understand, including you, what your best chance is."

*

Before bedtime, the dog needed to be walked.

The street lights had come on, and the early June night air was filled with sounds—birds, crickets—and the air smelled of newly mown sweet grass.

A jogger trotted by, looking tired but smiling in greeting.

That guy will probably sleep well tonight. Lucky bastard.

Normally, he tried to rush the dog through their evening walk, urging him to do his business in the tried-and-true spots so they could go back home.

Tonight, he took them blocks outside their usual route, keeping the conflicting voices out of his head.

The night smelled fresher to him than he could ever remember it smelling, but maybe that was only because he was noticing. Valuing every breath of free air.

*

"Carl and I are just meeting about your case," said Andrew, "so it's great you called."

"Last evening, I made up my mind."

There was a long pause.

"And?"

He looked around his office, hardly able to believe what he was about to say.

"I'm going to plead guilty."

"So, you're telling me you *are* guilty. That's how this has to go. That's what I need to hear you say to present this plea in court."

Explosions were going off inside his head.

"All right. I'll say it. Andrew, I am guilty."

"Good, we can move forward now."

"And we're going with simple negligence."

"We need to meet and discuss the details."

Dave set the receiver in its cradle and felt his pulse racing.

Had he just let himself be led into a bad decision by people, well-intentioned and otherwise?

He felt like he had just kicked himself hard in the gut.

*

Daisy and Jack's car was in the driveway when Dave got home from the office that day.

"Agent Murphy showed up with a warrant to search for your home computer," said Jack. "He seemed to think we had it in our possession."

"One of you two had to take it out of here. Do you know where it is now? Wait, don't tell me. Why is Murphy so hell-bent to find it?"

Jack danced around that.

"Who knows? Maybe he's hoping he'll find an ace to slip up the prosecutor's sleeve."

"But there's nothing on it for them to use against me. It's an old piece of junk, really."

Jack nodded.

Oh, it's better than that.

Chapter 16

Walking up the steps of the courthouse, Dave was struck by the ironies.

He was about to be tried by the government of a country that stood for freedom... and everything about his trial was a squeeze-play and a set-up.

You can't make this stuff up.

Two women waved to Hannah from the sidewalk nearby. They were holding up signs.

JUSTICE FOR DAVE MATTSON

INNOCENT

"Oh my gosh," said Hannah, "it's Bettina and Elise from work. I should say 'hi' and thank them for being here."

Bettina's face reddened a little as Hannah approached.

"There was going to be a bunch of us. We want to show the reporters how much support Dave has, but..."

"Most of the husbands said 'no' at the last minute," Elise said. "They're afraid their wives will be photographed and they'll come under suspicion, too."

"Everyone's scared."

Hannah squeezed their arms.

"Thank you for being brave enough to come out. It's terrible being pressured and terrorized by your own government when you've done nothing wrong."

*

Inside, the courtroom was half-filled with reporters, others entering pleas today, and assorted onlookers.

Daisy and Jack were already seated in the front row behind the defendant's table. She stood and kissed Dave on the cheek and Jack reached up to shake his hand, and Hannah took a seat beside them.

Across the aisle from the defendant's table sat the Assistant U.S. Attorney, a bear of a man Dave recognized from pictures as Constantin Malchik.

Third irony, Dave thought. *The prosecuting attorney came from Russia as a kid.*

Andrew Samson nodded at Malchik and said, as if reading Dave's mind, "Hard to believe that guy became All-American in football at Notre Dame. He looks like a K.G.B. agent."

"*All rise,*" the bailiff announced.

Judge Armfield Harkin entered from a door beside the judge's chair, seated himself, and struck the gavel twice.

"This court is now in session."

Dave noticed that Malchik was staring at him, his face blank but his eyes boring in. He shifted in his seat.

Harkin shuffled through some papers and, after a preliminary ramble, said, "In the case of the Government of the United States *versus* David Mattson, is the defendant present today?"

"He is," said Andrew, rising.

"And how does your client plead?"

Moment of truth, Dave thought, then reversed that. *More like a moment of bullshit.* He hated this game of gambling with his future. His life.

He stood. "I plead guilty, Your Honor."

A low murmur went through the section of reporters. Three rose and moved quickly out of the courtroom.

Judge Harkin checked his calendar.

"Since the government has asked to move these two cases along expeditiously, Dr. Abdullah's trial, in which you are a witness, Mr. Mattson, is set to begin on July one."

*

Outside, reporters thrust microphones at Dave and cameras were rolling.

"Mister Mattson, you pled guilty. Care to elaborate on that?"

"Give us a statement."

"What are you pleading guilty to?"

Hannah caught Bettina's and Elise's expressions. Both looked angry.

"We came here to support your husband."

"We believed you when you said he was innocent."

"But he admits he's guilty."

"We should never have come."

Andrew took Dave by the arm, and Carl grabbed Hannah's hand, pulling them through the throng of reporters.

"Let's go."

Dave slid into the backseat of Andrew's car. Stuffed into a trash can was Elise's sign, bent but still readable.

INNOCENT

Right.

His trial would begin on July first three days before Independence Day, the birthday of a nation that was about fairness and justice for all.

And there's the fourth irony.

*

'Liberty and justice for all,' Dave thought again, as they drove to the court early on July first. *I have to believe in our system*, one voice in his head insisted. Another said, *really—why?*

The courthouse foyer was filled with the hum of low voices when Andrew Samson met him.

"Stick to everything you told us. Malchik will come at you from every direction, ask the same question in different ways, trying to make you sound like you're contradicting yourself. Answer his questions exactly the same way each time."

Dave felt warm inside his suitcoat, shirt and necktie. He envisioned Malchik coming at him like the linebacker he had been at Notre Dame.

Malchik caught him staring, and smiled a cold smile.

In the courtroom, Yusuf Abdullah was seated at a table upfront with his lawyer. For just a moment, as Dave and Hannah were ushered in by Andrew to the first row of seats behind him, Abdullah turned and their eyes connected.

It was shocking to see how Abdullah had aged in the few months since the investigation had exploded into their lives. With their dark circles, his eyes looked hopeless.

As if he entered into a cloud bank, Dave sat in a kind of suspended state as the trial rolled into motion and only came out of it when Malchik's voice sounded, like a cannon going off, "Your Honor, I want to call David Mattson to the stand."

The onslaught began slowly.

"Mr. Mattson, would you please tell us how you came to know Yusuf Abdullah?"

"Dr. Abdullah came to me over twenty years ago and hired

me to be his Certified Public Accountant to help him with the tax returns for his medical practice."

"Were there any other services you rendered for Dr. Abdullah?"

"I represented him during an Internal Revenue Service audit about five years ago."

Malchik raised his eyebrows. "An audit." He looked at the jury. "What was the outcome of the audit?"

"The audit ended in a no change, even though the procedure became more of a criminal audit."

"A *criminal* audit," Malchik repeated for emphasis.

"Yes, but Dr. Abdullah was cleared of all charges."

"Did you have any reason to question his motives and actions when the investigation leaned toward criminal prosecution?"

"No. I actually held Dr. Abdullah to a higher trust level than most of my clients, as few taxpayers ever go through an audit so intense."

"I doubt this one will end the same, Mr. Mattson."

Dr. Abdullah's lawyer stood. "Objection. Prejudicing the jury."

"Sustained," Judge Harkin replied. "Mr. Malchik, present the facts of your case, not your opinions."

It was clear Malchik did not like that response.

"Are you aware that Dr. Abdullah has been indicted on more than thirty-five charges?"

"I am," Dave replied.

"Mr. Mattson, you have become deeply involved with Dr. Abdullah, and your relationship and your actions in filing the not-for-profit application for the Bread for Children have made you a potential co-conspirator."

He let the words hang in the air before continuing.

"He used his organization to send money to Iraq, in violation of the U.S. sanctions against that nation."

"But I had no idea that the organization was doing that. The application was the only thing I was involved in, and I had no knowledge of the transfer of funds to Iraq. I was told the monies raised were to go to Middle Eastern countries like Kuwait to feed refugees."

"You were told, and you went with that. As a professional with many years of experience, are you telling this court that you did not do a better job of looking into the background of the organization you were hired by Dr. Abdullah to help obtain a not-for-profit status?"

"I have no knowledge of when the monies you say were transferred, were transferred."

"I'm asking why you didn't trouble yourself to look into the organization's activities before legally associating yourself with it? Was there a reason you didn't want to know what was going on?"

"That wasn't the case. It was tax season, and there were other circumstances that demanded my attention. I have already pled guilty to negligence."

"Simple negligence. Isn't the truth that you had some knowledge, some awareness that Dr. Abdullah was doing something highly illegal, forbidden by federal law, and you *chose* not to look?"

"That's not true."

"But you ignored many red flags. Surely, in your line of work and with your experience, you can spot red flags. You told a federal agent that Dr. Abdullah pushed you hard to get the application through and did not supply information that was needed to complete that application, and you submitted it anyway. Was his pressuring you *not* a red flag?"

"As I said, I have pled guilty to negligence."

"Convenient," Malchik said in a low voice, just loud enough to be heard.

Andrew was on his feet. "Objection. Mr. Malchik is pushing his opinion again."

Malchik looked coldly at him.

"Facts, not commentary," said the judge.

"I was just trying to help Dr. Abdullah and his humanitarian cause," Dave offered.

"That was bad judgement on your part."

Both lawyers were on their feet. *"Your Honor."*

"Mr. Mattson, did you receive a letter from a prior accountant that Dr. Abdullah hired to complete the application for not-for-profit status prior to hiring you?"

"Yes."

"Did you later tell a federal agent that there were many disclosures in the letter that you ignored when you received it? You said, and I quote, "I did not pay sufficient attention to it?"

"Again, Your Honor," said Andrew, "my client has already said, twice, that he was negligent."

"What's your point, Mr. Malchik?" Judge Harkin pressed.

"Mr. Mattson seems to have lapses in either judgement or memory. I am making this point because the defense is likely to call him as their witness. I'm establishing that he is either totally unreliable or that there may be other motives beneath his so-called lapses."

"Why's he drilling me?" Dave asked, outside the courthouse during the lunch break. He had declined the offer of a quick bite at the café across the street.

"Look who the Devil dragged out of the dark," Andrew replied, before answering.

Agent Murphy was standing at the far end of the long, stone steps, smoking a cigarette and talking with Malchik. At the same moment, they looked across at Dave.

"I guess if they can't hang me, they have to prove I'm a liar or a lazy half-wit."

"We also have your sentencing to go through," said Andrew.

Dave startled. "Are you saying they can still come after me during sentencing?"

"It's possible."

"How bad can it be, considering I pled to a lesser infraction?"

"We'll have to see."

Back on the stand, the pressure did not let up.

"I'm referring again to the letter we discussed this morning, in which there is a reference to a prior organization."

"The source of the letter," Dave clarified, "was an unlicensed accountant who had turned the engagement of filling out the form into a full-blown audit." He added, "Preparation of the form was merely a gathering of information about the organization and transferring it to the form. No investigation is required by the Certified Public Accountant preparing the form. Dr. Abdullah had told me that the prior accountant was very difficult and that was why she was terminated. This letter confirmed that."

"Perhaps," Malchik said, looking at the jury, "but by ignoring the disclosures in the letter and answering the question on the form that Bread for Children was not an outgrowth of another entity was a falsehood. That was confirmed by you to your former staff person—let's see, her name is Mary—when she asked you about that."

Dave took a deep breath, seeing that Mary was now present and seated out in the courtroom. "I do not recall telling her it was a falsehood. I would not have approved either of us falsifying information."

"Are you saying that the information she gave to the government is false?"

Dave looked out at her, and she quickly looked away—and at the same time, he caught sight of Agent Murphy again.

"I don't know the circumstances or conditions in which she was interviewed. So, I can't say whether or not she was confused when she answered or... something else."

Murphy stared at him, then looked at Malchik with a faint smile.

He had no doubt Agent Murphy had pressured her, threatening prosecution.

When Dave finally stepped down, other witnesses were called to the witness stand.

Mary was not.

*

Evelyn was waiting for them on the courthouse steps the second morning of the trial.

"You shouldn't be here," Dave said. "You need to take care of yourself."

"Did Michael say something? I'm fine. I came to tell you face-to-face: be strong, David. The enemy always slips up, and I want to be on hand to see it when they do."

Andrew's oblique reference to a potential surprise at sentencing had kept him up most of the night. "I don't know."

A reporter stuck a microphone in Dave's face.

"Did you know Yusuf Abdullah was sending money to groups or nations hostile to America?"

Evelyn shoved the man's arm aside.

"Step back unless you want that microphone put where the sun doesn't shine." To the cameraman, she said, "I hope you got that. Make sure they run it on the evening news."

Well-intentioned as it was, this did nothing to lift Dave's spirits, and the atmosphere in the courtroom made it worse.

Dr. Abdullah sat with his face in his hands, half-slumped in his chair at a front table.

Dave stepped toward him, to offer support, to say he believed in him, but Andrew grabbed his arm.

"Not a good idea. Even though you gave positive testimony on his behalf, you're not on the same team anymore. It's every man for himself."

"Oh, that's just great."

"Did you not pick up the signals yesterday? Malchik and Murphy have their minds made up that, even if you're getting by with a lesser charge, they're going to stick it to you one way or another. Fraternizing with Yusuf is only going to ramp them up more."

Yusuf Abdullah's questioning was long and intense. Evidence was admitted and he was grilled for long stretches about each overseas contact, the lists of mosques and Islamic centers Murphy had found in the back of Dave's files at home, travel to Middle Eastern countries, and about emails that went to several recipients.

"Did you," Malchik asked, "send emails to David Mattson?"

"I did, yes. Time was of the essence for raising funds and I needed to be sure he was working on our postal permit."

"Did you or any of your associates have a friendship or a

social relationship—a connection—outside and apart from your business connection?"

"My wife and I attended his daughter's wedding."

"So, you were close, personal friends."

"I would not say that. As Mr. Mattson told you, he had helped me through a very difficult audit. We were, in that sense, on good terms. You could say friendly in the business, and since his daughter's wedding was, you might say, the event of the season, we were friendly in the social sense as well."

"When you emailed him, you contacted him at his office."

"Yes, of course."

Malchik looked at his notes and, for a split-second, made eye contact with Agent Murphy."

"Did you email him at his personal email address?"

Yusuf looked hesitant, as if he did not want to make a mistake.

"I don't recall."

"You don't recall."

"I do not."

"But you may have."

Yusuf looked at his lawyer, then at Dave.

"I do not recall."

*

Day two ended just before three, and Dave and Andrew walked quickly down the sidewalk, away from the court and reporters.

"What the hell was that about—all those questions about my personal email? Why was that brought into this again today?"

Andrew said nothing.

*

Day three of Yusuf Abdullah's trial made it plain that the government had enough evidence of wrongdoing. With almost forty charges against him, he was facing a lot of prison time.

As court adjourned and Yusuf was led out a side door in handcuffs, Judge Harkin signaled Andrew and Dave to approach the bench, also Malchik.

"I see no reason to delay sentencing for Mr. Mattson. It's been a long, grueling day. I want you all back here in court tomorrow at nine a.m., and I'll render my decision."

"I have something to present to you tomorrow, Your Honor," Malchik said quickly.

"Evidence that will affect sentencing?"

"Yes."

"Has it been entered into court records?"

"As of today, yes."

"I'll allow it."

*

Dave was shaken. "How can they admit evidence after I've already pled guilty?"

"Rules of jurisprudence. If the state or government has evidence that can affect sentencing, they can present it in judge's chambers on the day of sentencing."

"How is that fair if we can't know what it is ahead of time?"

Andrew placed his hand on Dave's shoulder.

"I've got this."

"Are you going to tell me *how* you've 'got this'?"

"No."

"Any idea what that evidence might be?"

"Some idea."

Chapter 17

They huddled together on the sidewalk on the street behind the courthouse, where there were no reporters.

Hannah and Daisy put their arms around Dave. Hannah was fighting back tears.

"Where's Jack?" he asked, a distraction, to help himself maintain composure.

"Parking the car. He'll be along shortly."

"I'd like to see him before…" Dave couldn't finish.

Sleepless last evening, he made the mistake of turning on the eleven o'clock news. The fourth story flashed a picture of him on the screen as the reporter said he was scheduled for sentencing in the morning.

"Judge Armfield Harkin has been presiding over both Mattson's and a related case, that of Dr. Yusuf Abdullah, who is accused of terrorist activities."

The other anchor added, "Harkin is known for issuing harsh sentences, isn't he?"

"That he is."

All night, Dave envisioned himself being sentenced and taken away in handcuffs.

"I'd like to see Jack before we go inside," he finished.

"He'll be along shortly."

Andrew Samson had come up.

"We should go in, Dave. Take a deep breath."

My last one as a free man?

Malchik was already in the courtroom, along with reporters, when Dave and Andrew entered.

Harkin entered and seated himself, then unfolded a single paper and laid it in front of himself.

"There is no need to drag this out, Mr. Mattson; I am ready to deliver your sentence. You have entered a plea of 'guilty' to a lesser charge of negligence, but as you know, this is a criminal case—and not only a criminal case, but one that involves criminality against the United States.

"Further, you should recall that this country is engaged in a war against terror. One that has claimed the lives of thousands of Americans. You, as well as I, can recall the images of jetliners being flown directly into the World Trade Center towers, and those buildings collapsing in twisted steel and rubble. The Pentagon was partially destroyed by another jetliner. We did not see the fourth plane crash land in a field in Pennsylvania, but we know that hundreds of other American lives were lost, preventing that jetliner from being used as another weapon against some other government structure.

He picked up a single sheet of paper. "Keep in mind the things I've just said when I read your sentence in a moment. I'll forewarn you that I'm not in the habit of going lightly in cases of this magnitude just because someone has pled to a lesser charge."

Dave's knees felt weak, and his mouth had gone dry.

"However, much as I hate to delay this, Mr. Malchik here has asked to present evidence that may affect your sentence. And he may do so at this time. Mr. Malchik?"

Malchik cleared his throat.

"Someone will be here momentarily, Your Honor. I'm not sure what the delay is, but I promise it will not be long."

Slipping his cell phone out of his pocket, he texted.

Where the hell are you?

*

Agent Murphy felt the cell phone buzz in his pocket and ignored it.

"Excuse me, gentlemen," he said to the two men who were blocking his entrance to the court. One was carrying a shoulder bag. "I'm late."

"We know," said Jack. "We're here to ask if you really want to go through with what you're about to do."

Murphy tried to push past them, and the two men pushed together shoulder-to-shoulder.

"Get the hell out of my way."

The one with the shoulder bag said, "We know what you're planning to do and…"

"This is bullshit. *Move*," Murphy said, shoving him aside.

The bag slammed into the courtroom door, loudly.

"*Keep your hands off him*," Jack shouted.

*

Judge Harkin furrowed his brow and he called out, "Bailiff, there seems to be a problem outside my courtroom. Please see what the commotion is and put a stop to it."

When the bailiff opened the door, three men were standing there, looking like fists might fly.

Agent Murphy said angrily, "These men are trying to keep

me from entering, Your Honor, with the evidence we need to present."

"With evidence," said one of them, "that will likely influence you to level a harsh sentence against my father-in-law, David Mattson."

David had moved to where he could see out into the entryway.

"Jack? What are you doing? You're interrupting."

"I should interrupt. *We* should interrupt," he said, indicating the man with him. The judge needs to see what we have to show him."

Judge Harkin was turning red.

"I'm going to call every bailiff in the building and have you two removed."

Jack stepped inside the courtroom and stood his ground.

"Please, Your Honor. If you don't see this, a gross miscarriage of justice may be committed here today."

"Your Honor," Malchik insisted, "if you don't call the bailiffs, I will. These men are trying to prevent our presentation of evidence and breaking the law right at this moment by impeding the execution of my duties as an officer of the law. I'm placing you two under arrest."

As Murphy reached for Jack's arm, Jack stepped away from his grasp.

"You're trying to present *falsified* evidence," Jack shot back.

A loud murmur from the reporters ran through the courtroom.

Judge Harkin leapt to his feet.

"Follow me into my chambers. All of you. *Now*."

*

"Judge Harkin," said Jack, "we know what Agent Murphy has in his pocket—a data stick with emails he or someone else working for the government planted in Dave Mattson's computer."

Malchik's face had turned shades of red.

"Judge, have these men taken away? The U.S. Government wants to present—"

Andrew interrupted him, "present evidence you created, to guarantee that my client could still be sent to prison, even after admitting to a lesser crime."

Malchik's fists were doubled, but before he could speak again, Harkin intervened.

"You'll speak when I ask you to." He sat down heavily behind his desk.

Malchik looked furious. "I am an Assistant U.S. Attorney."

"That may well be, but this is my office. And frankly, after the dictates that have been coming down to us judges, telling us how to run our courts, I'm a little low on patience with you guys." He pointed at Agent Murphy. "What do you have?"

Murphy held up a small metal object. "I have here a USB flash drive. On it, we have emails and other documents that were sent to David Mattson's personal email address. They're filled with plans to move money on behalf of Yusuf Abdullah's organization to entities in this country that have been identified as possible terrorist organizations or supporters of them. Also, other plans to circumvent the system to legitimize Abdullah's storefront operations."

Dave was coming out of his skin.

"That's a *lie*."

Andrew grabbed his arm. "I told you I've got this.

"Your Honor, I have two men here who have information

you need to hear. This is Mr. Mattson's son-in-law, Jack, and this gentleman is an expert in computer forensics. I believe," Andrew said, turning to Murphy. "You actually know this man, because you've relied on his services before as an expert witness," he added. "Isn't that right?"

"Hello, Agent Murphy, Peter Ellis. I'm certain you remember me. We've worked together, what—six or seven times?"

Murphy looked uneasy and did not reply.

"Why are you gentlemen here?" Judge Harkin asked. "And remember, you're *only* here by my good graces. Whatever you have to say that's interrupting this sentencing had better be of utmost importance."

Peter Ellis slid the shoulder bag he had been carrying off onto the edge of the judge's desk and pulled out a laptop computer.

"I'll swear under oath that emails and files were uploaded onto this computer, Mr. Mattson's, by an outside source. I'm willing to stake my reputation as an expert government witness with whom you have worked on several occasions, Agent Murphy, that the files you have on your USB drive are the same files. Except that…"

He paused to let the gravity of the moment sink in.

"Except that, I can show Judge Harkin the files on this laptop were uploaded *after* the laptop was removed from Mr. Mattson's home by his son-in-law, to have it serviced. Provable because they're date and time-stamped. It was never returned to him, because what was found in his emails and on his hard drive were items planted there. And so, it was decided—by Jack here, with my strong advice—to keep the computer out of Mattson's possession. In short, he did not have this computer with him at any time after these items were planted, and Jack will testify to that."

Murphy started to speak, but Ellis kept going.

"Further, I can show that except for one or two files I opened to check, none of the others were *ever* opened by *anyone*, which is a second proof Mr. Mattson had never seen them, much less originated or responded to them."

Judge Harkin held up his hand.

"Are you saying, and are you willing to testify under oath as you offered, that the U.S. Government planted documents in this man's laptop?"

"That is what I'm saying."

Malchik had become livid.

"I want that laptop opened and turned on," he said, loudly, "and I want you to see the files and emails in question. The government has worked hard to prove our claim that Mr. Mattson is a half-step shy of being a full-blown traitor to this country. You need to see exactly what this man was up to and punish him for supporting enemies of this country, an involvement he's trying to minimize by pleading to a namby-pamby claim of 'negligence.'"

He had moved quickly to the judge's desk and was starting to flip open the laptop.

Harkin pushed the lid of the computer down forcefully, and bore down on Peter Ellis.

"Let me get this right. You're saying the U.S. Government engaged in or sanctioned the setting up of an American citizen, Mr. Mattson, to pressure him for his testimony against Yusuf Abdullah and/or to set him up for a harsh sentence. And you say, you're *sure*. How?"

Ellis looked directly at Murphy.

"With the help of other experts in cyber security and internet fraud, we were able to obtain the IP address from which the emails and files were sent.

"We know exactly where the things planted in Mattson's computer originated."

Harkin pointed at Dave, Jack, Peter Ellis, Andrew, and then at Agent Murphy.

"You gentlemen, step out into the corridor behind my office and close the door behind you. Stand thirty feet apart if that will keep you from brawling. I want a few minutes with Mr. Malchik."

*

Even with the heavy office door closed, they could hear raised voices. Agent Murphy had taken the judge's advice and walked down the end of the corridor alone.

Dave said to Jack in a low voice, "You took the laptop out of my house, didn't you? You found Ellis here and whoever else discovered what they'd done."

Jack nodded. "That's right."

"You probably saved my butt."

"Possibly," said Ellis.

"What do you mean 'possibly'?"

Ellis glanced down the hallway to be sure Murphy was at a good distance, and lowered his voice even more.

"The laptop in there is yours, but it's a zombie. The hard drive is wiped clean and your personal IP address has been eliminated. That in itself took a miracle of technology. We did it to prevent whoever perpetrated this from downloading more files into it and to wipe out your laptop completely in case somehow

Murphy figured Jack had it and came to him with a warrant."

Dave looked at Jack and Andrew. "Why didn't you guys tell me about any of this?"

"We had to keep you in the dark," said Andrew, "in case you were questioned under oath. But that's not what you should be concerned about at this moment."

Ellis added, "If Malchik persuades the judge to look into your files and emails and Harkin sees there's nothing there, we're in very hot water. All of us. Me included."

"Wait, you insinuated that you knew that Murphy or someone close to him did this. You said you tracked the IP address."

"Look," Ellis went on, "I saw the files and that, as soon as they were opened, they would be logged into your computer's memory as if you'd opened them in the months before the investigation started. The couple I looked at were coded to do that. Proving that you were in on some illegal scheme. Amazingly devious.

"But the address they came from…"

Ellis grinned. "A bluff. I looked at Murphy when I said I knew exactly where the files originated. The fact is, I didn't—not until I saw his expression when I said that. He's guilty as hell and he really doesn't want to be exposed."

Dave ran his hand wildly through his hair.

"So now we just have to wait and see if Harkin allows Malchik to open my computer."

Ellis, Jack, and Andrew were silent.

*

In ten minutes, the judge's office door opened.

Malchik emerged quickly into the corridor, ignoring Dave and the others. Ignoring even Murphy, who saw him and followed swiftly, the sound of their heels echoed in the corridor until they reached the stairway and descended together out of sight.

Judge Harkin stepped out.

"Mr. Mattson, I'd like you and your counsel to come in. You can allow these other gentlemen in, as well, if you like. They may want to hear what I have to say."

When they were seated around Harkin's desk, he remained on his feet, pacing, looking out the window, then looking at them.

"The rhetoric I just heard goes like this. In the course of fighting a war, sometimes the 'good guys' have to push the limits to win.

"Sometimes, for instance, a sheriff's deputy or State Trooper profiles a young driver as a 'possible criminal' because young people are widely known to use recreational drugs. They pull a young person over on the highway for, let's say, having a tail light out. Then the officer pressures that young person into stepping from their vehicle so they can perform a search of the car. Most of the time, this is done without a warrant, which, make no mistake, is illegal, in that it violates our constitutional rights. This illegal action on the part of law enforcement is very often viewed as justifiable because we've declared a so-called 'war on drugs, and, well, the thinking is that the end justifies the means, because a significant percentage of the time drugs are found. A young 'criminal' has been apprehended."

Dave hoped he knew where this was going.

"I'm afraid that courts—judges—have allowed and even rewarded such actions on the part of our officers in the field. We know what a lot of danger and resistance they face daily. We know their job is tough and they deal with actual, hardened criminals a lot. Their lives are on the line constantly. So, we—I'll say it—look the other way when legal boundaries are stepped over.

"Now we have the no-knock warrant, which allows officers to, essentially, break into homes, weapons drawn, sometimes firing. Again, using the rhetoric that we've become a very violent society, with criminals armed to the teeth and ready to shoot and kill cops."

Harkin stopped pacing and looked straight at Dave.

"But there are times when the government way oversteps the bounds and a judge has to say, 'Not this time.' There is uncovering information, and there is planting false information. The end hoped for does not justify the means."

Dave felt a wave of relief rising.

"I sent Mr. Malchik packing after I took apart not only his methods but his personal character. He wanted to bury you because he thought he could and that it would somehow win him and his superiors' points with those even farther up the chain. I don't know if what I said—that this kind of criminality is, in my opinion, actionable—sank into his skull. I doubt it. He strikes me as a true, right-wing 'believer' one who will always insist the end justifies everything they do to 'win.' And unfortunately, he has Washington behind him.

"But are we still America if we 'win' some battles at the cost of what we stand for?"

Dave could not keep from responding.

"You're restoring my faith in this country, Your Honor. I have to admit, it was wavering."

"I wish I could let you off the hook completely, Mr. Mattson, now that I've learned what's been done to you. But given that you did plead guilty to a lesser charge, by the way, you should thank your lawyers for their counsel. I am going to sentence you now. Please go back out to the courtroom. I will follow in a minute. If you think I'm letting you off with nothing, you're wrong."

Dave looked at Andrew and Jack. Had he spoken too soon?

*

"I'm giving you one-year probation," Judge Harkin announced to the courtroom.

A murmur rose again, and Harkin rapped his gavel twice.

"The next reporter who opens his or her mouth will be banned indefinitely. See how your news manager likes that. Now, Mr. Mattson," he continued.

"You'll report every week to an officer of the court. And you'll do a year of community service."

He rapped his gavel again and stood.

"The court is adjourned."

Over the sound of foot shuffling and quiet talk, Harkin motioned to Dave to approach the bench.

"There are public libraries and senior and youth programs that can use help. I suspect you'll meet some people who are, like yourself, just good people.

"Now, if you'll excuse me, I want to prepare a carefully worded statement for the press. They'll be hounding me, and I need to say something that doesn't get me investigated and explains why you're, essentially, being exonerated of all the accusations."

Dave felt like his chest was bursting and he leapt to his feet. Where were Hannah, Daisy, and Jack?

When the small group of supporters that had gathered on a quiet side of the building saw him emerge, grinning ear to ear, a cheer went up.

Hannah and Daisy threw their arms around him, tears rising, and Jack stood back to give them space. Jen and Cliff, Les and Louise Thackery clapped him on the back. Evelyn clasped her hands together and raised them high in a gesture of victory.

"Congratulations."

"Cause for celebration."

"You're a good man. We all know it."

"Apparently, the judge does, too."

Dave looked out from them and up at the sky. Was the air fresher, clearer?

He kissed Hannah on the cheek again. "Where's Evelyn? I thought I saw her."

Daisy looked around.

"She was just here."

Coming down the building's front steps, Malchik was surrounded by a throng of reporters, with Agent Murphy following silently behind him.

"You're not going to tell us what the sentence was?" One reporter pressed Malchik.

"Are you unhappy about today's ruling?"

"Sounds like David Mattson was more or less let off the hook—is that right?"

Malchik reached the sidewalk and stopped. His voice was hostile.

"America is plagued with liberal judges; that's all I can say.

Today was a travesty."

One reporter laughed.

"Judge Harkin—a *liberal*? He's one of the toughest judges when it comes to sentencing…"

Agent Murphy felt a tug on his sleeve.

An old woman had pushed herself close and was glaring at him.

"You're an evil, evil little man. You should be exposed for what you are. I don't care that you think you're serving this country. You're not. Men like you are working against real justice."

He was done with the crowd of gabbling, shouting reporters. Done with Malchik's browbeating and threats. And no interest in engaging this old woman.

"Excuse me," he said. Trying to push her.

"*No*. I don't excuse you. Let me tell you something—and you're going to stand your ground and listen."

She had hold of his sleeve now.

"Years ago, the U.S. Government, your employer, did a terrible thing. It went after many innocent people they labeled as Communists and enemies of the State, and destroyed them whether they were guilty of that charge or not."

He tried to tug his arm away from her.

"I'm not finished. People lost their jobs and their homes. People died. Are you listening to me? People *died* and families were left to grieve forever because of what men like you do."

Murphy jerked his sleeve from her grasp.

"Walk away, *coward*. Plug your ears to keep from hearing the truth, which is that many, many of us out here know you're not patriots. You've destroyed that word. You've trampled the rule of law and you're the criminals."

"Can you live with that?" she shouted after him. "*Can you?*"

*

Hannah handed Dave her cell phone.

"It's your father."

"Dad! Best news possible. The judge is preparing a statement for the press that clears me of all the worst parts of what the government tried to pin on me. And no problem dealing with the easy sentence he handed me."

"Evelyn must feel some sense of vindication," his father said.

A quirky remark.

"I suppose so. Why do you say that?"

"Her family has kept this secret for many years because, back in the day, such things brought shame and disgrace to people. Stupid, I know, but that's the way people thought back then."

"What things brought shame and disgrace? What are you talking about?

"Evelyn may not be happy, I told you. To this day, it plagues her. I promised never to speak of it to anyone, but, well, today I just have to. When the government destroyed her father, he went into a long, slow decline. Then came the deep depression. Evelyn was so young and she's the one who found him…"

Dave saw her coming around the corner of the building. She had on her face the bright look of someone who had, after terrible losses and many years, just experienced a very dear and personal kind of victory.

Printed in the USA
CPSIA information can be obtained
at www.ICGtesting.com
LVHW090154080924
790362LV00009B/46

9 781835 430866